Lydia could feel heat hover between their mouths in a slow tease before they first met.

Then they met.

And all that had been missing was suddenly there.

At first taste she was Raul's, and he knew for her hands moved to the back of his head and he kissed her back as hard as her fingers demanded.

He slid one arm around the waist to move her body from the wall and closer into his, so that her head could fall backward.

If there was a bed, she would be on it.

If there was a room, they would close the door.

Yet there wasn't, and so he halted them, but only their lips.

"What do you want to do?" he whispered into her skin, and then blew on her neck, damp from his kisses. Then he raised his head and met her eyes. "Tonight I can give you anything you want."

Dear Reader,

This is my 100th title for Harlequin!

Rather than use this space to tell you about Raul and Lydia, I would like to thank you.

Whether it is the first or hundredth time you have read my books, I am so grateful to my readers.

Even if we haven't met face-to-face or online, hopefully we've shared some time through words on a page, and shared a smile or three when one of my heroes misbehaves.

Or one of my heroines messes up. They tend to do that a lot.

I often cry when I'm writing, but I laugh often, too.

I hope, in some way, my stories let you do the same.

Happy reading and love always.

Carol xxxx

Carol Marinelli

THE INNOCENT'S SECRET BABY

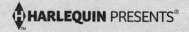

HARLEQUIN PRESENTS®

Rom
M

Recycling programs
for this product may
not exist in your area.

ISBN-13: 978-0-373-06047-4

The Innocent's Secret Baby

First North American publication 2017

Copyright © 2017 by Carol Marinelli

HARLEQUIN®
www.Harlequin.com

Printed in U.S.A.

Carol Marinelli recently filled in a form asking for her job title. Thrilled to be able to put down her answer, she put "writer." Then it asked what Carol did for relaxation and she put down the truth— "writing." The third question asked for her hobbies. Well, not wanting to look obsessed, she crossed her fingers and answered "swimming"—but given that the chlorine in the pool does terrible things to her highlights, I'm sure you can guess the real answer!

Books by Carol Marinelli

Harlequin Presents

His Sicilian Cinderella
Sicilian's Shock Proposal

One Night With Consequences

The Sheikh's Baby Scandal

The Billionaire's Legacy

Di Sione's Innocent Conquest

Irresistible Russian Tycoons

The Price of His Redemption
The Cost of the Forbidden
Billionaire Without a Past
Return of the Untamed Billionaire

Harlequin Medical Romance

Their Secret Royal Baby

The London Primary Hospital

Playboy on Her Christmas List

Desert Prince Docs

Seduced by the Sheikh Surgeon

Visit the Author Profile page at Harlequin.com for more titles.

For Lena,

my mum.

You were wonderful as both
and I will love you forever.

Until we meet again...

PROLOGUE

SURELY NOT?

As Raul Di Savo thanked the mourners who had attended his mother's funeral a figure standing in the distance caught his attention.

He wouldn't *dare* to come here!

Not today of all days.

The tolling of the bell in the small Sicilian church had long since ceased, but it still seemed to ring in Raul's ears.

'Condoglianze.'

Raul forced himself to focus on the elderly gentleman in front of him rather than the young man who stood on the periphery of the cemetery.

'Grazie,' Raul said, and thanked the old man for his attendance.

Given the circumstances of Maria's death, and fearing Raul's father's wrath, most had stayed away.

Gino had not attended his wife's funeral.

'She was a whore when I married her and she goes into the ground the same.'

That was how he had broken the news of her death to his son.

Raul, having been told of a car accident involving

his mother, had travelled from Rome back to Casta—a town on the Sicilian wild west coast—but he had arrived only to be told that she had already gone.

He had been too late.

Slowly, painfully, he had pieced together the timeline of shocking events that had led to Maria's death. Now Raul performed his familial duties and stood graveside as the line of mourners slowly moved past him.

Condolences were offered, but small talk was strained. The events of the last few days and the savage condemnations that were now coursing through the valley made even the simplest sentence a mockery.

'She was a good…' A lifetime family friend faltered in his choice of words. 'She was…' Again there was hesitation over what should be said. 'Maria will be missed.'

'She will be,' Raul duly replied.

The scent of freshly dug soil filled his nostrils and lined the back of his throat, and Raul knew there was no comfort to be had.

None.

He had left it too late to save her.

And now she was gone.

Raul had studied hard at school and had done so well in his exams that he had received a scholarship and, as he had always intended, been able to get out of the Valley of Casta.

Or, as Raul and his friend Bastiano had called it, *the Valley of Hell.*

Raul had been determined to get his mother away from his father.

Maria Di Savo.

Unhinged, some had called her.

'Fragile' was perhaps a more appropriate word.

Deeply religious until she had met his father, Maria had hoped to join the local convent—an imposing stone residence that looked out on the Sicilian Strait. His mother had wept when it had closed down due to declining numbers, as if somehow her absence had contributed to its demise.

The building had long stood abandoned, but there was not a day Raul could remember when his mother hadn't rued the day she had not followed her heart and become a novice nun.

If only she had.

Raul stood now, questioning his very existence, for her pregnancy had forced Maria into the unhappiest of marriages.

Raul had always loathed the valley, but never more so than now.

He would never return.

Raul knew his drunken father's demise was already secured, for without Maria's care his descent would be rapid.

But there was another person to be taken care of.

The man who had forced this tragic end.

Raul had made a vow as he'd thrown a final handful of soil into his mother's open grave that he would do whatever it might take to bring him down.

'I shall miss her.'

Raul looked up and saw Loretta, a long-time friend of his mother's who worked in the family bar.

'No trouble today, Raul.'

Raul found himself frowning at Loretta's choice of words and then realised why she suddenly sounded concerned—he was looking beyond the mourners now, to the man who stood in the distance.

Bastiano Conti.

At seventeen, Bastiano was a full year younger than Raul.

Their families were rivals.

Bastiano's uncle owned most of the properties and all of the vineyards on the west of the valley.

Raul's father was king of the east.

The rivalry went back generations, and yet their black history had been ignored by the young boys and, growing up, the two of them had been friends. They had gone through school together and often spent time with each other during the long summer breaks. Before Raul had left the valley he and Bastiano had sat drinking wine from the opposing families' vines.

Both wines were terrible, they had agreed.

Similar in looks, both were tall and dark and were opposed only in nature.

Bastiano, an orphan, had been raised by his extended family and got through life on charm.

Raul was serious and mistrusting and had been taught to be fickle.

He trusted no one but said what he had to to get by.

Though different in style, they were equally adored by women.

Bastiano seduced.

Raul simply returned the favour.

There had been no rivalry between the young men—both could have their pick of the valley and the fruits were plenty.

Yet Bastiano had used his dark charm on the weakest and had taken Maria as his lover.

Pillow talk had been gathered and secrets had been prised from loose lips.

Not only had Maria had an affair—she had taken it beyond precarious and slept with a member of the family that Gino considered his enemy.

When the affair had been discovered—when the rumours had reached Gino—Loretta had called her to warn her Gino was on his angry way home. Maria had taken out a car she didn't know how to drive.

An unwise choice in the valley.

And Raul knew the accident would not have happened but for Bastiano.

'Raul…' Loretta spoke softly, for she felt the tension rip through him and could hear his ragged breathing. She held on to his hand, while knowing nothing could really stop him now. 'You are Sicilian, and that means you have a lifetime to get your revenge—just don't let it be today.'

'No,' Raul agreed.

Or did he refute?

Raul's words were coming out all wrong, his voice was a touch hoarse, and as he looked down he could see the veins in his hand and feel the pulse in his temples. He was primed for action, and the only thing Raul knew for sure was that he hated Bastiano with all that he had.

He dropped Loretta's hand and brushed past her, then shrugged off someone else who moved to try to stop him.

'Raul!' The priest shot him a warning. 'Not here— not now.'

'Then he should have stayed away!' Raul responded

as he strode through the cemetery towards the man who had sent his mother to an early grave.

Raul picked up speed—and God help Bastiano because hate and fury catapulted Raul those last few steps.

'Pezzo di merda...' Raul shouted out words that did not belong in such a setting.

Any sane man who saw murder approach would surely turn and run, but instead Bastiano walked towards Raul, hurling insults of his own. 'Your mother wanted—'

Raul did not let him finish, for Bastiano had already sullied her enough, and to silence him Raul slammed his fist into Bastiano's face. He felt the enamel of Bastiano's tooth pierce his knuckle, but that was the last thing he felt.

It was bloody.

Two parts grief, several belts of rage and a hefty dose of shame proved a volatile concoction indeed.

Raul would kill him.

That was all he knew.

Yet Bastiano refused to go quietly and fought back.

There were shouts and the sounds of sirens in the distance as the two men battled it out. Raul felt nothing as he was slammed against a gravestone. The granite tore through the dark suit and white shirt on his back with the same ease that it gouged through muscle and flesh.

It didn't matter.

His back was already a map of scars from his father's beatings, and adrenaline was a great anaesthetic.

Only vaguely aware of the wound that ran from

shoulder to flank, Raul hauled himself up to stand, took aim again and felled his rival.

Yet Bastiano refused to submit.

Raul pinned Bastiano and slammed his fist into his face, marring those perfect features with relish, and then he held him to the ground and told him he should have stayed the hell away from his mother.

'Like *you* did!'

Those words were more painful than any physical blow, for Raul knew that he had done just that—stayed away.

CHAPTER ONE

Rome again… Rome again…

The City of Love.

Wrapped in a towel, and damp from the shower, Lydia Hayward lay on the bed in her hotel suite and considered the irony.

Yes, she might be in Rome, and meeting tonight with a very eligible man, but it had nothing to do with love.

There were more practical matters that needed to be addressed.

Oh, it hadn't been said outright, of course.

Her mother hadn't sat her down one evening and explained that, without the vast and practically bottomless pit of money that this man could provide, they would lose everything. *Everything* being the castle they lived in, which was the family business too.

And Valerie had never *said* that Lydia had to sleep with the man she and her stepfather were meeting tonight.

Of course she hadn't.

Valerie *had*, however, enquired whether Lydia was on the Pill.

'You don't want to ruin your holiday.'

Since when had her mother taken an interest in such things? Lydia had been to Italy once before, on a school trip at the age of seventeen, and her mother hadn't been concerned enough to ask then.

Anyway, why would she be on the Pill?

Lydia had been told to 'save' herself.

And she had.

Though not because of her mother's instruction—more because she did not know how to let her guard down.

People thought her aloof and cold.

Better they think that than she reveal her heart.

And so, by default, she had saved herself.

Lydia had secretly hoped for love.

It would seem not in this lifetime.

Tonight she would be left alone with him.

The towel fell away and, though she was alone, Lydia pulled it back and covered herself.

She was on the edge of a panic attack, and she hadn't had one since…

Rome.

Or was it Venice?

Venice.

Both.

That awful school trip.

She had said yes to this trip to Rome, hoping to lay a ghost to rest. Lydia wanted to see Rome through adult eyes, yet she was as scared of the world now as she had been as a teenager.

Pull yourself together, Lydia.

And so she did.

Lydia got up from the bed and got dressed.

She was meeting Maurice, her stepfather, at eight

for breakfast. Rather than be late she just quickly combed her long blonde hair, which had dried a little wild. She had bought a taupe linen dress to wear, which had buttons from neck to hem—though perhaps not the best choice for her shaking hands.

They are not *expecting you to sleep with him!*

Lydia told herself she was being utterly ridiculous even to entertain such a thought. She would stop by for a drink with this man tonight, with her stepfather, thank him for his hospitality and then explain that she was going out with friends. Arabella lived here now and had said they should catch up when Lydia got here.

In fact...

Lydia took out her phone and fired off a quick text.

Hi, Arabella,
Not sure if you got my message.
Made it to Rome.
I'm free for dinner tonight if you would like to catch up.
Lydia

And so to breakfast.

Lydia stepped out of her suite and took the elevator down to the dining room. As she walked through the lavish foyer she caught sight of herself in a mirror. Those deportment classes had been good for something at least—she was the picture of calm and had her head held high.

Yet she wanted to run away.

'No, grazie.'

Raul Di Savo declined the waiter's offer of a second espresso and continued to read through reports on the Hotel Grande Lucia, where he now sat, having just taken breakfast.

At Raul's request his lawyer had attained some comprehensive information, but it had come through only this morning. In a couple of hours Raul was to meet with Sultan Alim, so there was a lot to go through.

The Grande Lucia was indeed a sumptuous hotel, and Raul took a moment to look up from his computer screen and take in the sumptuous dining room that was currently set up for breakfast.

There was the pleasant clink of fine china and a quiet murmur of conversation and, though formal, the room had a relaxed air that had made Raul's stay so far pleasurable. There was a certain old-world feel to the place that spoke of Rome's rich history and beauty.

And Raul wanted the hotel to be his.

Raul had been toying with the idea of adding it to his portfolio and had just spent the night in the Presidential Suite as a guest of Sultan Alim.

Raul hadn't expected to be so impressed.

He had been, though.

Every detail was perfection personified—the décor was stunning, the staff were attentive yet discreet, and it appeared to be a rich haven for both the business traveller and the well-heeled tourist.

Raul was now seriously considering taking over this landmark hotel.

Which meant that so too was Bastiano.

Fifteen years on and their rivalry continued unabated.

Mutual hatred was a silent, yet daily motivator—a black cord that connected them.

And Bastiano would be arriving later today.

Raul knew that Bastiano was also a personal friend of Sultan Alim. Raul had considered if that might have any bearing on their negotiations but had soon discounted it. Sultan Alim was a brilliant businessman, and his friendship with Bastiano would have no sway over his dealings, Raul was certain of that.

Raul rather hoped his presence at the hotel might cause Bastiano some discomfort, for though they moved in similar circles in truth their paths rarely crossed. Raul, even on his father's death, had never returned to Casta.

There had been no respects to pay.

Yet Casta had remained Bastiano's base.

He had converted the old convent into a luxury retreat for the seriously wealthy.

It was actually, Raul knew, an extremely upmarket rehab facility.

His mother would be turning in her grave.

Raul's black thoughts were interrupted when the portly middle-aged gentleman sitting to his right made his disgruntled feelings known.

'Who do you have to sleep with around here to get some service?' he muttered in well-schooled English.

It would seem that the tourists were getting impatient!

Raul smiled inwardly as the waiter continued to ignore the pompous Englishman. The waiter had had enough. This man had been complaining since the moment he had been shown to his table, and there was absolutely nothing to complain about.

Raul was not being generous in that observation. Many of his nights were spent in hotels—mainly those that he owned—and so more than most he had a very critical eye.

There were certain ways to behave, and despite his accent this man did not adhere to them. He seemed to assume that just because he was in Rome no one would speak English and his insults would go unnoticed.

They did not.

And so—just because he could—Raul gestured with his index and middle fingers towards the small china cup on his table. The motion was subtle, barely noticeable to many, and yet it was enough to indicate to the attentive waiter that Raul had changed his mind and would now like another coffee.

Raul knew that his preferential treatment would incense the diner to his right.

From the huff of indignation as his drink was delivered, it did.

Good!

Yes, Raul decided, he wanted this hotel.

Raul read through the figures again and decided to make some further calls to try to get behind the real reason the Sultan was selling such an iconic hotel. Even with Raul's extensive probing he could see no reason for the sale. While the outgoings were vast, it was profitable indeed. The crème de la crème stayed at the Grande Lucia, and it was here that their children were christened and wed.

There had to be a reason Alim was selling, and Raul had every intention of finding out just what it was.

Just as Raul had decided to leave he glanced up and saw a woman enter the dining room.

Raul was more than used to beautiful women, and the room was busy enough that he should not even have noticed, but there was something about her that drew the eye.

She was tall and slender and she wore a taupe dress. Her long blonde hair appeared freshly washed and tumbled over her shoulders. Raul watched as she had a brief conversation with the maître d' and then started to walk in his direction.

Still Raul did not look away.

She made her way between the tables with elegant ease, and Raul noted that she carried herself beautifully. Her complexion was pale and creamy, and suddenly Raul wanted her to be close enough so that he could know the colour of her eyes. She lifted a hand and gave a small wave, and Raul, who was rarely the recipient of a sinking feeling where women were concerned, felt one now.

She was with *him*, Raul realised—she was here to have breakfast with the obnoxious man who sat to his right.

Pity.

The blonde beauty walked past his table, and he could not help but notice the delicate row of buttons that ran from neck to hem on her dress. But he pointedly returned his attention to his computer screen rather than mentally undress her.

That she was with someone rendered her of no interest to him in that way.

Raul loathed cheats.

Still, the morning scent of her was fresh and heady—a delicate cloud that reached Raul a few seconds after she had passed and lingered for a few moments more.

'Good morning,' she said as she took a seat, and unlike her companion's the woman's voice was pleasant.

'Hmph.'

Her greeting was barely acknowledged by the seated Englishman. Some people, Raul decided, simply did not know how to appreciate the finer things in life.

And this lady was certainly amongst the finest.

The waiter knew that too.

He was there in an instant to lavish attention upon her and was appreciative of her efforts when she attempted to ask for Breakfast Tea in schoolgirl Italian, remembering her manners and adding a clumsy *'per favour'*.

Such poor Italian would usually be responded to in English, in arrogant reprimand, and yet the waiter gave a nod. *'Prego.'*

'I'll have another coffee,' the man said and then, before the waiter had even left, added rather loudly to his companion, 'The service is terribly slow here— I've had nothing but trouble with the staff since the moment I arrived.'

'Well, I think it's excellent.' Her voice was crisp and curt, instantly dismissing his findings. 'I've found that a please and a thank-you work wonders—you really ought to try it, Maurice.'

'What are your plans for today?' he asked.

'I'm hoping to do some sightseeing.'

'Well, you need to shop—perhaps you should consider something a little less beige,' Maurice added. 'I asked the concierge and he recommended a hair and beauty salon a short distance from the hotel. I've booked you in for four.'

'Excuse me?'

Raul was about to close his laptop. His interest had waned the second he had realised she was with someone.

Almost.

But then the man spoke on.

'We're meeting Bastiano at six, and you want to be looking your best.'

The sound of his nemesis's name halted Raul and again the couple had his full attention—though not by a flicker did he betray his interest.

'*You're* meeting Bastiano at six,' the blonde beauty responded. 'I don't see why I have to be there while you two discuss business.'

'I'm not arguing about this. I expect you to be there at six.'

Raul drained his espresso but made no move to stand. He wanted to know what they had to do with Bastiano—any inside knowledge on the man he most loathed was valuable.

'I can't make it,' she said. 'I'm meeting a friend tonight.'

'Come off it!' The awful man snorted. 'We both know that you don't have any friends.'

It was a horrible statement to make, and Raul forgot to pretend to listen and actually turned his head to see her reaction. Most women Raul knew would crumble a little, but instead she gave a thin smile and a shrug.

'Acquaintance, then. I really am busy tonight.'

'Lydia, you will do what is right by the family.'

Her name was Lydia.

As Raul continued to look at her, perhaps sensing her conversation was being overheard, she glanced over and their eyes briefly met. He saw that they were china blue.

His question as to the colour of her eyes was answered, but now Raul had so many more.

She flicked her gaze away and the conversation was halted as the waiter brought their drinks.

Raul made no move to leave.

He wanted to know more.

A family had come into the restaurant and were being seated close to them. The activity drowned out the words from the table beside him, revealing only hints of the conversation.

'Some old convent...' she said, and the small cup in his hand clattered just a little as it hit the saucer.

Raul realised they were discussing the valley.

'Well, that shows he's used to old buildings,' Maurice said. 'Apparently it's an inordinate success.'

A baby that was being squeezed into an antique high chair started to wail, and Raul frowned in impatience as an older child loudly declared that he was hungry and he wanted chocolate milk.

'*Scusi...*' he called to the waiter, and with a mere couple of words more and a slight gesture of his hand in the family's direction his displeasure was noted.

Noted not just by the waiter—Lydia noted it too.

In fact she had noticed him the moment the maître d' had gestured to where her stepfather, Maurice, was seated.

Even from a distance, even seated, the man's beauty had been evident.

There was something about him that had forced her attention as she had crossed the dining room.

No one should look that good at eight in the morning.

His black hair gleamed, and as she had approached Lydia had realised it was damp and he must have been in the shower around the same time as her.

Such an odd thought.

That rapidly turned into a filthy one.

Her first with the recipient in the same room!

She had looked away quickly as soon as she had seen that he was watching her approach.

Her stomach had done a little somersault and her legs had requested of their owner that they might bypass Maurice and be seated with *him*.

Such a ridiculous thought, for she knew him not at all.

And he *wasn't* nice.

That much she knew.

Lydia turned her head slightly and saw that on his command the family was being moved.

They were *children*, for goodness' sake!

This man irritated her.

This stranger irritated her far more than a stranger should, and she frowned her disapproval at him and her neck felt hot and itchy as he gave a small shrug in return and then closed his computer.

You were already leaving, Lydia wanted to point out. *Why have the family moved when you were about to leave?*

Yes, he irritated her—like an itch she needed to scratch.

Her ears felt hot and her jaw clenched as the waiter came and apologised to him for the disruption.

Disruption?

The child had asked for chocolate milk, for goodness' sake, and the baby had merely cried.

Of course she said nothing. Instead Lydia reached for her pot of tea as Maurice droned on about their plans for tonight—or rather, what he thought Lydia should wear.

'Why don't you speak to a stylist?'

'I think I can manage. I've been dressing myself since I was three,' Lydia calmly informed him, and as she watched the amber fluid pour into her cup she knew—she just knew—that the stranger beside her was listening.

It was her audience that gave her strength.

Oh, she couldn't see him, but she knew his attention was on her.

There was an awareness between them that she could not define—a conversation taking place such as she had never experienced, for it was one without words.

'Don't be facetious, Lydia,' Maurice snapped.

But with this man beside her Lydia felt just that.

The sun was shining, she was in Rome, and the day stretched before her—she simply did not want to waste a single moment of it with Maurice.

'Have a lovely day…' She took her napkin and placed it on the table, clearly about to leave. 'Give Bastiano my regards.'

'This isn't up for debate, Lydia. You're to keep tonight free. Bastiano has flown us to Rome for this meeting and housed us in two stunning suites. The very least you can do is come for a drink and thank him.'

'Fine,' Lydia retorted. 'But know this, I'll have a drink, but it's not the "very least" I'll do—it's the most.'

'You'll do what's right for the family.'

'I've tried that for years,' Lydia said, and stood up. 'I think it's about time I did what's right by *me*!'

Lydia walked out of the restaurant with her head still high, but though she looked absolutely in control she was in turmoil, for her silent fears were starting to come true.

This wasn't a holiday.

And it wasn't just drinks.

She was being offered up, Lydia knew.

'Scusi...'

A hand on her elbow halted her, and as she spun around Lydia almost shot into orbit when she saw it was the man from the next table.

'Can I help you?' she snapped.

'I saw you leaving suddenly.'

'I wasn't aware that I needed your permission.'

'Of course you don't,' he responded.

His voice was deep, and his English, though excellent, was laced heavily with a rich accent. Her toes attempted to curl in her flat sandals at its sound.

Lydia was tall, but then so was he—she didn't come close to his eye level.

It felt like a disadvantage.

'I just wanted to check that you were okay.'

'Why wouldn't I be?'

'I heard some of what was said in there.'

'And do you *always* listen in on private conversations?'

'Of course.' He shrugged. 'I rarely intervene, but you seemed upset.'

'No,' Lydia said. 'I didn't.'

She knew that as fact—she was very good at keeping her emotions in check.

She should have walked off then. Only she didn't. She continued the conversation. 'That baby, however, *was* upset—and I didn't see you following him across the dining room.'

'I don't like tantrums with my breakfast, and the toddler is now throwing one,' he said. 'I thought I might go somewhere else to eat. Would you like to join me?'

He was forward *and* he lied, for she had seen the waiter removing his plates and knew he had already had breakfast.

'No, thank you.' Lydia shook her head.

'But you haven't eaten.'

'Again,' Lydia replied coolly, 'that's not your concern.'

Bastiano *was* his concern, though.

For years revenge had been his motivator, and yet still Bastiano flourished.

Something had to give, and Raul had waited a long time for that day to arrive.

Now it would seem that it had—in the delicate shape of an English rose.

Raul was no fool, and even from the snippets of conversation he'd heard, he had worked out a little of what was going on.

Bastiano wanted Lydia to be there tonight.

And Lydia didn't want to go.

It was enough to go on—more than enough. For despite her calm demeanour he could see the pulse leaping in her throat. More than that, Raul knew women—and knew them well.

There was another issue that existed between them.

She was turned on.

So was he.

They had been on sight.

From her slow walk across the dining room and for every moment since they had been aware of each other at the basest of levels.

'Come for breakfast,' he said, and then he remembered how she liked manners. *'Per favore.'*

Lydia realised then that every word she had uttered in the restaurant had been noted.

It should feel intrusive.

And it did.

But in the most delightful of ways.

Her breath felt hot in her lungs and the warm feeling from the brief touch of his hand on her arm was still present.

She wanted to say yes—to accept this dark stranger's invitation and follow this dangerous lead.

But that would be reckless at best, and Lydia was far from that.

There was something about him that she could not quite define, and every cell in her body recognised it and screamed danger. He was polished and poised—immaculate, in fact. And yet despite the calm demeanour there was a restless edge. Beneath the smooth jaw was a blue hue that hinted at the unshaven, decadent beauty of him. Even his scent clamoured for attention, subtle and at the same time overwhelming.

Raul had her on the edge of panic—an unfamiliar one.

He was potent—*so* potent that she wanted to say yes. To simply throw caution to the wind and have breakfast with this beautiful man.

She didn't even know his name.

'Do you always ask complete strangers for breakfast?' Lydia asked.

'No,' he admitted, and then he lowered his head just a fraction and lowered his voice an octave more. 'But then you defy the hour.'

CHAPTER TWO

THEY DEFIED THE HOUR, Lydia thought. Because as they stepped outside the hotel surely the moon should be hanging in a dark sky.

It was just breakfast, she told herself as his hand took her elbow and guided her across the busy street.

Yet it felt like a date.

Her first.

But it wasn't a romantic Italian evening, for the sun shone brightly and Rome was at its busy rush hour best.

Yet he made it so.

The restaurant he steered her to had a roped-off section and the tables were clearly reserved, yet the greeter unclipped the rope and they breezed through as if they were expected guests.

'Did you have a reservation?' Lydia asked, more than a little confused as they took their seats.

'No.'

'Then…' Lydia stopped, for she had answered her own question—the best seats were permanently re-served for the likes of him. He had a confident air that demanded, without words, only the best.

Coffee was brought and sparkling water was poured.

They were handed the heavy menus, but as the waiter started to explain the choices he waved him away.

Lydia was grateful that he had, for there was a real need for the two of them to be left alone.

He was an absolute stranger.

A black-eyed stranger who had led and she had followed.

'I don't know your name,' Lydia said, and found she was worried a little that it might disappoint.

'Raul.'

It didn't.

He rolled the *R* just a little, and then she found herself repeating it, *'Rau—el...'* Though it did not roll easily from her tongue.

She waited for his surname.

It didn't come.

'I'm Lydia.'

'I had worked that out.' He glanced down at the menu. He never wasted time with small talk, unless it suited him. 'What would you like?'

She should be hungry. Lydia hadn't eaten since the plane, and even then she had just toyed with her meal.

She had been sick with nerves last night, but now, though still nervous, the feeling was pleasant.

'I'd like...' Lydia peered at the menu.

Really she ought to eat something, given that breakfast was the reason she was here.

But then she blushed while reading the menu, because food was the furthest thing from her mind.

'It's in Italian,' Lydia said, and could immediately have kicked herself, for it was such a stupid thing to say—and so rude to assume it should be otherwise.

But he did not chide her, and he did not score a point by stating that Italy was, in fact, where they were.

He just waited patiently as she stumbled her way through the selections till she came upon something she knew. But she frowned. 'Tiramisu for breakfast?'

'Sounds good.'

Perhaps he hadn't heard the question in her voice, because Lydia had assumed it was served only as a dessert, but Raul was right—it sounded good.

The waiter complimented their choice as he took their orders, and very soon she tasted bliss.

'Oh...' It was light and not too sweet, and the liquor made it decadent. It really had been an accidental perfect choice.

'Nice,' Raul said, and watched her hurriedly swallow and clear her mouth before speaking.

'Yes.' Lydia nodded. 'Very.'

'I wasn't asking a question.'

Just observing.

He looked at her mouth, and Lydia wondered if she had a crumb on her lip, but she resisted putting out her tongue to check.

And then he looked at her mouth, and the pressure within built as still she resisted that simple oral manoeuvre. Instead she pulled her bottom lip into her mouth and ran her tongue over it there.

No crumb.

Her eyes met his and she frowned at his impertinence as they asked a question—*Are you imagining what I think you are?*

Of course she said no such thing, and his features were impassive, but those black eyes offered his response.

Yes, Lydia, I am.

Had she had her purse with her, Lydia might well have called for the bill and fled, because she felt as if she were going insane. She looked around. Almost certain that the spectacle she was creating would have the world on pause and watching.

Yet the waiters were waiting, the patrons were chatting, the commuters were commuting and the word was just carrying on, oblivious to the fire smouldering unchecked in this roped-off section.

And so too must Raul be—oblivious, that was. For his voice was even and his question polite. 'How are you finding Rome?'

Lydia was about to nod and say how wonderful it was, or give some other pat response, but she put down her spoon, let go of the end of her tether and simply stated the truth.

The real reason she was in Rome.

'I'm *determined* to love it this time.'

'Okay...' Raul said. His stance was relaxed and he leant back in the seat, seemingly nonchalant, but in his mind he was searching for an angle—how to get her to speak of Bastiano without too direct a question.

Lydia was terribly formal—very English and uptight. One wrong move, Raul knew, and he would be the recipient of a downed napkin and he'd have to watch her stalk off back to the hotel.

She was so incredibly sexy, though.

A woman who would make you *earn* that reward.

Lydia did not flirt, he noted.

Not a fraction.

No playing with her hair, no leaning forward, no secret smiles and no innuendo.

Really, the way she was sitting so upright in the chair, he could be at a breakfast meeting with Allegra, his PA.

Except Raul was aroused.

He was here to garner information, Raul reminded himself, and took his mind back to their conversation.

Or tried to.

'How long are you here for?'

'Till Sunday,' Lydia answered. 'Two nights. How about you?'

'I'm here for business.'

Raul should not be taking this time now. He had a very packed day. First he would meet with Alim and his team. Then, if time allowed, he would drop in unexpectedly on the other hotel he owned in Rome.

But he always made Bastiano his business.

'When do you leave?' she asked.

'When business is done.' Raul's jet was in fact booked for six this evening, but he did not share his itinerary with anyone outside his close circle. 'So, you've been to Rome before?'

'Yes, I came to Italy on a school trip and had a rather miserable time. I don't think my mood then did the place justice.'

'Where did you go?'

'Rome, Florence and Venice.'

'Which was your favourite?'

Lydia thought for a moment. 'Venice.'

'And your least favourite?'

Oh, that was easy—Lydia didn't have to think to

answer that, even if he didn't understand her response. 'Venice.'

He *did* understand.

So much so that Raul again forgot that he was trying to steer the conversation. Even though Bastiano was the reason Raul was there, for now he left Raul's mind.

He thought of Venice—the city he loved and now called home.

Not that he told *her* that.

Raul gave away nothing.

Then suddenly he did.

For as she looked over she was rewarded with the slow reveal of his smile.

And his smile was a true and very rare gift.

She saw those full dark lips stretch and the white of his teeth, but the real beauty was in eyes that stared so deeply into hers she felt there was nowhere to hide.

And nor did she want to.

'Venice,' Raul said, in that deep, measured voice, 'can be the loneliest place in the world.'

'Yes,' Lydia admitted. 'It was.'

It was as if she was seventeen again, walking alongside the Grand Canal alone and wanting to be in love with the city.

To be in love.

Of course nearly every schoolgirl on a trip to Italy secretly hoped for a little romance.

But on that day—on that terribly lonely day— Lydia would have been happy with a friend.

One true friend.

Raul was right. Lydia had felt utterly alone then, and for the most part she had felt the same since.

She was looking at him, but not really, and then his voice brought her back.

'And you forgive her because how could you not?'

'Her?' Lydia checked, her mind still on friendships that had failed.

'Venice.'

'I wasn't there long enough to forgive her,' Lydia admitted.

'What happened?'

'Just being a teenager…'

She could easily dismiss it as that, but it had been more. Oh, she didn't want to tell him that her father had just died and left behind him utter chaos, for while it might explain her unhappiness then, it wasn't the entire truth—it had been more than that.

'Schoolgirls can be such bitches.'

'I don't think it is exclusive to that age bracket.'

'No!' Lydia actually laughed at his observation because, yes, those girls were now women and probably still much the same.

She glanced at her phone, which had remained silent.

Arabella hadn't responded to her text.

Neither had she responded to Lydia's last message.

And suddenly Lydia was back in Italy, hurting again.

'What happened in Venice?'

Raul chose his moment to ask. He knew how to steer conversations, and yet he actually found himself wanting to know.

'We went to Murano…to a glass factory.' She shook her head and, as she had then, felt pained to reveal the truth.

It felt like a betrayal.

Money should never be discussed outside the home.

'And…?' Raul gently pushed.

Why lie? Lydia thought.

She would never see him again.

It wasn't such a big deal.

Surely?

'My father had died the year before.'

He didn't say he was sorry—did not offer the automatic response to that statement.

It was oddly freeing.

Everyone had been *so* sorry.

If there's anything I can do… The words had been tossed around like black confetti at his funeral.

Yet they had done nothing!

When it was clear the money had gone, so had they.

'I'd told Arabella, my best friend, that my mother was struggling financially.' Lydia was sweating, and that wasn't flattering. She wanted to call the waiter to move the shade umbrella but knew she could be sitting in ice and the result would be the same.

It wasn't sexy sweat.

Lydia wasn't turned on now.

She felt sick.

'I told Arabella that we might lose the castle.'

She offered more explanation.

'The castle was in my mother's family, but my father ran it. I thought he had run it well, but on his death I found out that my parents had been going under.'

Raul offered no comment, just let her speak.

'He took his own life.'

She'd never said it out loud before.

Had never been allowed to say it.

'I'm sorry you had to go through that.'

And because he hadn't said sorry before, now—when he did—she felt he meant it.

'I still can't believe he left me.'

'To deal with the fallout?'

He completed her sentence, even though Lydia thought she already had. She thought about it for a moment and nodded.

'Things really were dire. My mother kept selling things off, to pay for my school fees. The trip to Italy was a compulsory one. I got a part-time job—saved up some spending money. Of course it didn't come close to what my friends had. They were hitting all the boutiques and Arabella kept asking why I wasn't buying anything. In the end I told her how bad things were. I swore her to secrecy.'

He gave a soft, mirthless laugh—one that told her he understood.

And then they were silent.

In *that* moment they met.

Not at a breakfast table in Rome but in a bleak, desolate space a world away from there.

They met and he reached across and took her hand, and together they walked it through.

'At the factory, after a demonstration, everyone was buying things. I held back, of course. There was a table with damaged glassware and Belinda, another friend, held up a three-legged horse and suggested it was something that I might be able to afford. I realised then that Arabella had told everyone.'

She could still feel the betrayal.

Could still remember looking over to her best friend as everyone had laughed.

Arabella hadn't so much as blushed at being caught.

'She suggested that they all have a whip-round for me.'

'So you walked off?' Raul asked, impatient to know and understand her some more.

'Oh, no!' Lydia shook her head and then sighed. 'I used up all my spending money, and the money I'd been given for my birthday, and bought a vase that I certainly couldn't afford.'

It was that response in herself she had hated the most.

'How shallow is that?'

'People have been known to drown in shallow waters.'

'Well, it's certainly not easy to swim in them! Anyway, I didn't see them much after that...'

'You left school?'

'I went to the local comprehensive for my final year. Far more sensible...but hell.'

Everything—not just the fact that she was a new girl for the last year, but every little thing, from her accent to her handwriting—had ensured she didn't fit in from the very first day.

Raul knew it would have been hell.

He could imagine *his* schoolmates if an Italian version of Lydia had shown up in his old schoolyard. Raul could guess all she would have gone through.

'I was a joke to them, of course.'

He squeezed her hand and it was the kindest touch, so contrary to that time.

'Too posh to handle?' Raul said, and she nodded, almost smiled.

But then the smile changed.

Lydia never cried.

Ever.

Not even when her father had died.

So why start now?

Lydia pulled her hand back.

She was done with introspection—done with musings.

They hurt too much.

Lydia was somewhat appalled at how much she had told him.

'Raul, why am I here?'

'Because…' Raul shrugged, but when that did not appease her he elaborated. 'Maurice was getting in the way.'

Lydia found herself laughing, and it surprised her that she could.

A second ago she had felt like crying.

It was nice being with him.

Not soothing.

Just liberating.

She had told another person some of the truth and he had remained.

'Maurice is my stepfather,' she explained.

'Good,' Raul said, but she missed the innuendo.

'Not really.'

Lydia didn't respond to his flirting as others usually did, so he adopted a more businesslike tone. The rest they could do later—he wanted information now.

'Maurice wants you to be at some dinner tonight?'

Lydia nodded. 'He's got an important meeting with a potential investor and he wants me there.'

'Why?'

Lydia gave a dismissive shake of her head.

She certainly wasn't going to discuss *that*!

'I probably shan't go,' Lydia said, instead of explaining things. 'I'm supposed to be catching up with a friend—or rather,' she added, remembering all he had heard, 'an acquaintance.'

'Who?'

'Arabella.' She was embarrassed to admit it after all she had told him. 'She works in Rome now.'

'I thought you fell out?'

'That was all a very long time ago,' Lydia said, but she didn't actually like the point he had raised.

They hadn't fallen out.

The incident had been buried—like everything else.

She conversed with Arabella only through social media and the odd text. It had been years since they had been face-to-face, and Lydia wasn't sure she was relishing the prospect of seeing her, so, rather than admit that, she went back to his original question—why Maurice wanted her to be there tonight.

'The family castle is now a wedding venue.'

'Do you work there?'

Lydia nodded.

'Doing what?'

'I deal with the bookings and organise the catering…' She gave a tight smile, because what she did for a living was so far away from her dreams. When her father had been alive she had loved the visitors that came to the castle. He would take them through it and pass on its rich history and Lydia would learn something new every time.

'And you still live at home?'

'Yes.'

She didn't add that there was no choice. The business was failing so badly that they couldn't afford much outside help, and she didn't get a wage as such.

'Bastiano—this man we're supposed to meet tonight—has had a lot of success converting old buildings… He has several luxury retreats and my mother and Maurice are hoping to go that route with the castle. Still, it would take a massive cash injection…'

'Castles need more than an injection—they require a permanent infusion,' Raul corrected.

All old buildings did.

It galled him that Bastiano had been able to turn the convent into a successful business venture. On paper it should never have worked, and yet somehow he had ensured that it had.

'Quite,' Lydia agreed. 'But more than money we need his wisdom…' She misinterpreted the slight narrowing of Raul's eyes as confusion. 'A lot of these types of venture fail—somehow Bastiano's succeed.'

'So why would this successful businessman be interested in *your* castle?'

Lydia found she was holding her breath. His question was just a little bit insulting. After all, the castle was splendid indeed, and Raul could have no idea what a disaster in business Maurice had turned out to be.

'I'm sure Bastiano recognises its potential.'

'And he wants you there tonight so he can hear your vision for the castle?'

Lydia gave a small shake of her head. The truth was that she was actually *opposed* to the idea of turning it into a retreat—not that her objections held much weight.

'Then why do you need to go?'

'I've been invited.'

'Lydia, I have had more business meetings than I've had dinners.' Raul spoke when she did not. 'But I can't ever remember asking anyone—*ever*—to bring along their daughter, or rather their stepdaughter.'

She blushed.

Those creamy cheeks turned an unflattering red.

Lydia knew it—she could feel the fire, not just on her skin but building inside her at the inappropriateness he was alluding to.

'Excuse me?' she snapped.

'Why?' Raul said. 'What did you do?'

'I mean you're rude to insinuate that there might be something else going on!'

'I know that's what you meant.'

He remained annoyingly calm, and more annoyingly he didn't back down.

'And I'm not *insinuating* anything—I'm telling you that unless you hold the deeds to the castle, or are to be a major player in the renovations, or some such, there is no reason for this Bastiano to insist on your company tonight. '

'He isn't insisting.'

'Good.' Raul shrugged. 'Then don't go.'

'I don't have any excuse not to.'

'You don't need one.'

It was Lydia who gave a shrug now.

A tense one.

She was still cross at his insinuation.

Or rather she was cross that Raul might be right—that he could see what she had spent weeks frantically trying *not* to.

'Lydia, can I tell you something?'

She didn't answer.

'Some free advice.'

'Why would I take advice from a stranger?'

'I'm no longer a stranger.'

He wasn't. She had told him more than she had told many people who were in her day-to-day life.

'Can I?' Raul checked.

She liked it that he did not give advice unrequested, and when she met his eyes they were patient and awaiting her answer.

'Yes.'

'You can walk away from anyone you choose to, and you don't have to come up with a reason.'

'I know that.'

She had walked off from breakfast with Maurice, after all.

It wasn't enough, though—Lydia knew that. And though Raul's words made perfect sense, they just did not apply to her world.

'So why don't you tell your stepfather that you can't make it tonight because you're catching up with a friend?'

'I already have.'

'But you don't like Arabella,' Raul pointed out. 'So why don't you meet me instead?'

She laughed a black laugh. '*You're* not a friend.'

He wasn't.

'No,' he answered honestly. 'I'm not.'

She was about to take a sip of her coffee when he added something else.

'I could be for tonight, though.'

'I don't think so.' Lydia gave a small laugh, not really getting what he had just said—or rather not really thinking he meant it.

'Do you have many friends?' she asked, replacing her cup. Perhaps her question was a little invasive, but she'd told him rather a lot and was curious to know about him.

'Some.'

'Close friends?' Lydia pushed.

'No one whose birthday I need to remember.'

'No one?'

He shook his head.

'I guess it saves shopping for presents.'

'Not really.'

Raul decided to take things to another level and tell her how things could be. In sex, at least, he was up front.

'I like to give a present the morning after.'

Lydia got what he meant this time.

She didn't blush. If anything Lydia felt a shiver, as if the sun had slipped behind a cloud.

It hadn't.

He was dark, he was dangerous, and he was as sexy as hell. Absolutely she was out of her depth.

'I'm here to sightsee, Raul.'

'Then you need an expert.'

Lydia stared coolly back at this man who was certainly that. She wondered at his reaction if she told him just how inexperienced she was—that in fact he would be her first.

Not that it was going to happen!

But *what* a first, Lydia thought.

She went to reach for water but decided against it, unsure she could manage the simple feat when the air thrummed with an energy that was foreign to her.

He was potent, and Lydia was tempted in a way she had never been.

She glanced down to his hand, and that was beautiful too—olive-skinned and long-fingered with very neat nails. And it was happening again, because now she imagined them inside her.

Oh!

She was sitting at breakfast, imagining those very fingers in the filthiest of thoughts, and she dared not look up at him for she felt he could read her mind.

'So what are your plans for today?' Raul asked.

His voice seemed to be coming from a distance, and yet he was so prominent in her mind.

She could take his hand, Lydia was certain, and be led to his bed.

Oh, what was *happening* to her?

'I told you—sightseeing, and then I'm shopping for a dress.'

'I wish I could be there to see that.'

'I thought men didn't like shopping.'

'I don't, usually.'

His eyes flicked to the row of buttons at the front of her dress and then to the thick nipples that ached, just *ached* for his touch, for his mouth. And then they moved back to her face.

'I have to go,' Raul told her, and she sat still as he stood. With good reason: her legs simply refused to move. Standing would be difficult...walking back over to the hotel would prove a completely impossible feat.

Please go, Lydia thought, because she felt drunk on lust and was trying not to let him see.

He summoned the waiter, and though he spoke in Italian he spoke slowly enough that she could just make out what was being said.

Hold this table for tonight at six.

And then he turned to where she sat, now with her back to him, and lowered his head. For a moment she thought he was going to kiss her.

He did not.

His breath was warm on her cheek and his scent was like a delicious invasion. His glossy black hair was so close that she fought not to reach out and feel it, fought not to turn and lick his face.

And then he spoke.

'Hold that thought till six.'

Lydia blinked and tried to pretend that she still felt normal, that this was simply breakfast and she was somehow in control.

'I already told you—I can't make it tonight.'

Then he offered but one word.

'Choose.'

CHAPTER THREE

WHAT THE HELL was happening to her?

Lydia watched him walk across the street and then disappear inside the hotel.

He did not turn around. He didn't walk with haste.

She wanted him to hurry, to disappear, just so that she could clear her mind—because in fact she *wanted* him to turn around.

One crook of his finger and she knew she would rise and run to him—and that was so *not* her. She kept her distance from people—not just physically but emotionally too.

Her father's death had rocked every aspect of her world, and the aftermath had been hell. Watching her mother selling off heirlooms and precious memories one by one, in a permanent attempt to keep up appearances, and then marrying that frightful man. Finding her friends had all been fair-weather ones had also hurt Lydia to the core. And so she held back—from family, from friends and, yes, from men.

She was guarded, and possibly the assumption made by others that she was cold was a correct one.

But not now—not this morning.

She felt as if she had been scalded, as if every

nerve was heated and raw, and all he had done was buy her breakfast.

She sat alone at the table. There was nothing to indicate romance—no candles or champagne—and no favourable dusk to soften the view. Just the brightness of morning.

There had been no romance.

Raul had offered her one night and a present the following morning. She should have damn well slapped him for the insult!

Yet he'd left her on a slightly giddy high that she couldn't quite come down from.

Sightseeing as such didn't happen.

When she should have been sorting out what to do about tonight she wandered around, thinking about this morning.

But finally she shopped, and accepted the assistant's advice, and stood in the changing room with various options.

The black did not match her mood.

The caramel felt rather safe.

But as for the red!

The rich fabric caressed her skin and gave curves where she had few. It was ruched across her stomach and her hand went to smooth it before she realised that was the desired effect—it drew the eye lower.

Lydia slipped on the heels that stood in the corner and looked at her reflection from behind. And then she looked from the front.

She felt sexy, and for the first time beautiful and just a touch wild as she lifted her hair and imagined it piled up in curls. And *his* reaction.

It wasn't Bastiano's reaction she was envisaging—it was the reaction of the man who had invited her out this evening.

Only that wasn't quite right.

He hadn't asked her out on a date.

Raul had invited her to a night in his bed.

'Bellisima...'

Lydia spun around as the assistant came in, and her cheeks matched the fabric as if she had been caught stealing.

'That dress is perfect on you...' the assistant said.

'Well, I prefer this one.'

She could see the assistant's confusion as she plucked the closest dress to hand and passed it to her.

Caramel—or rather a dark shade of beige.

Safe.

Bastiano was *not* a safe option.

Raul knew that as fact.

'I trust you were comfortable last night?' Sultan Alim asked when they met.

Raul had met the Sultan once before, but that had been in the Middle East and then Alim had been dressed in traditional robes. Today he wore a deep navy suit.

'Extremely comfortable,' Raul agreed. 'Your staff are excellent.'

'We have a rigorous recruiting process for all levels.' Alim nodded. 'Few make it through the interviews, and not many past the three-month trial. We retain only the best.'

Raul had seen that for himself.

Alim was unhurried as he took Raul behind the

scenes of his iconic hotel. 'I have had four serious expressions of interest,' Alim went on to explain. 'Two I know have the means—one I doubt. The other...' He held his hand flat and waved it to indicate he was uncertain.

'So I have one definite rival?' Raul said, and watched as Alim gave a conceding smile.

Both knew Raul was a serious contender.

He didn't have to try hard to guess who the other was—not that Alim let on.

Raul had done his homework, and he knew that Alim was not just an astute businessman but very discreet in all his dealings.

He would have to be.

Allegra, Raul's long-suffering PA, had found out all she could on him.

Sultan Alim was a playboy, and his palace's PR must be on overtime to keep his decadent ways out of the press.

Alim kissed but never told, and in return the silence of his aggrieved lovers was paid for in diamonds.

And in business he played his cards close to his chest.

The latter Raul could attest to, for Alim did not bend to any of Raul's mercurial ways.

By the end of a very long day Raul was still no closer to finding out the real reason for the sale.

Alim had dismissed his team and was taking Raul for one final look around.

'I haven't seen Bastiano,' Raul commented as the elevator arrived to take them down to the function rooms. When Alim did not respond, Raul pushed. 'I see that his guests are already here.'

Still Alim gave nothing away. 'I shall take you now to the ballroom.'

Raul had no choice but to accept his silence.

He knew that Alim and Bastiano were friends, and in turn Alim would know that Raul and Bastiano were business rivals and enemies.

So, instead of trying to find out more about Bastiano, Raul returned his mind to work.

'Why?' Raul asked Sultan Alim as they walked along the lush corridors. 'Why are you selling?'

'I've already answered that,' Sultan Alim said. 'I am to marry soon and I am moving my portfolio back to the Middle East.'

'I want the real reason.'

Alim halted mid-stride and turned to face Raul as he spoke.

'You have several hotels throughout Europe that you aren't letting go, yet this jewel you are.'

'You're correct,' Alim said. 'Hotel Grande Lucia *is* a jewel.'

As Raul frowned, Alim gave a nod that told Raul he would explain some more.

'Come and see this.'

They stepped into the grand ballroom, where a dark-haired woman, dressed in a dark suit that was rather too tight, was standing in the middle of the dance floor.

Just standing.

Her shoes must be a little tight too, for she was holding stilettos in one hand.

'Is everything okay, Gabi?' Alim asked her.

'Oh!' Clearly she hadn't heard them come in, because she startled but then pushed out a smile. 'Yes, everything is fine. I was just trying to work out the table plan for Saturday.'

'We have a large wedding coming up,' Alim explained to Raul.

'And both sets of parents are twice divorced.' Gabi gave a slight eye-roll and then chatted away as she bent to put on her shoes. 'Trying to work out where everyone should be seated is proving—'

'Gabi!' Alim scolded, and then turned to Raul. 'Gabi is not on my staff. *They* tend to be rather more discreet.' He waved his hand, but this time it was to dismiss her. 'Excuse us, please.'

Alim, who had until now been exceptionally pleasant with all his staff, was less than polite now. Raul watched as a very put-out Gabi flounced from the ballroom.

'She is a wedding planner from an outside firm,' Alim said, to explain the indiscretion. '*My* staff would *never* discuss clients that way in front of a visitor.'

'Of course.' Raul nodded as the huge entrance doors closed loudly, and he resisted raising his eyebrows as the crystals in the chandeliers responded to the pointed slam.

It was actually rather spectacular to watch.

The reflection of the low, late-afternoon sun was captured by several thousand crystals, and for a moment it was as if it was raining sunbeams as light danced across the walls and the ceiling and the floor— even over their suits.

'It's a beautiful ballroom,' Raul commented as he looked around, though he was unsure exactly why Alim had brought him here instead of to a meeting room, when it was figures that Raul wanted to discuss.

'When I bought the hotel those had not been cleaned in years,' Alim said, gesturing to the magnificent lights. 'Now they are taken down and cared for properly. It is a huge undertaking. The room has to be closed, so no functions can be held, and it is all too easy to put it off.'

Raul could see that it would be, but he did not get involved in such details and told Alim so.

'I leave all that to my managers to organise,' Raul said.

Alim nodded. 'Usually I do too, but when I took over the Grande Lucia there had been many cost-cutting measures. It was slowly turning into just another hotel. It is not just the lighting in the ballroom, of course. What I am trying to explain is that this hotel has become more than an investment to me. Once I return to my homeland I shall not be able to give it the attention it deserves.'

'The next owner might not either,' Raul pointed out.

'That is his business. But while the hotel is mine I want no part in her demise.'

Raul knew he was now hearing the true reason for the sale. To keep this hotel to its current standard would be a huge undertaking, and one that Raul would play no major part in—he would delegate that. Perhaps he'd do so more carefully, given what he had been told. But at the end of the day managers managed, and Raul had neither the time nor the inclination to be that heavily involved.

'Now you have given me pause for thought,' Raul admitted.

'Good.' Alim smiled. 'The Grande Lucia deserves

the best caretaker. Please,' Alim said, indicating that their long day of meetings had come to an end, 'take all the time you need to look around and to enjoy the rest of your stay.'

Sultan Alim excused himself and Raul stood in the empty ballroom, watching the light dancing around the walls like a shower of stars.

He thought of home.

And he understood Alim's concerns.

Last year Raul had purchased a stunning Venetian Gothic *palazzo* on the Grand Canal.

It required more than casual upkeep.

The house was run by Loretta—the woman who had warned his mother of Gino's imminent return home all those years ago.

She ran the staff—and there were many.

Raul looked around the ballroom at the intricate cornices and arched windows.

Yes, he knew what Alim was talking about. But this was a hotel, not a home.

Raul would play no part in her demise.

He was going to pass.

So there was no need to linger.

His mind went back to that morning and he hoped very much that Lydia would be there to meet him tonight—not just to score a point over Bastiano and to rot up his plans.

Raul had enjoyed her company.

His company was not for keeps.

Lydia knew that.

She sat in her button-up dress in the hairdresser's at four and asked for a French roll, but the hairdresser tutted, picked up a long coil of blonde and suggested—or rather, *strongly* suggested—curls. After some hesitation finally Lydia agreed.

Whatever had happened to her this morning, it was still occurring.

She felt as if she were shedding her skin, and at every turn she fought to retrieve it.

Her lashes were darkened, and then Lydia opened her eyes when the beautician spoke.

'*Porpora...*'

Lydia did not know that word, but as the beautician pushed up a lipstick Lydia managed, without translation, to work out what it meant.

Crimson.

'No.' Lydia shook her head and insisted on a more neutral shade.

Oh, Lydia wanted to be back in her cocoon—she was a very unwilling butterfly indeed—but she did buy the lipstick, and on her way back to the hotel she stopped at the boutique and bought the red dress.

And then she entered the complex world of sexy shoes.

Lydia had bought a neutral pair to go with the caramel dress and thought she was done. But...

'Red and red,' the assistant insisted.

'I think neutral would look better.'

'You *need* these shoes.'

Oh, Lydia *was* starting to take advice from strangers for she tried them on. They were low-heeled and slender and a little bit strappy.

'It's too much,' Lydia said, but both women knew she was not protesting at the price.

'No, no,' the assistant said. 'Trust me—these are right.'

Oh, Lydia didn't trust her.

But she bought them anyway.

For *him*.

Or rather to one day dress up alone to the memory of him.

As she arrived back at the hotel Lydia looked at the restaurant across the street, to the roped-off section and the table he had reserved for them.

Of course he wasn't there yet.

Yet.

Knowing he would be—knowing she *could* be—made tonight somehow worse.

Her mother called, but she let it go to voicemail.

A pep talk wasn't required.

Lydia didn't need to be told that everything hinged on tonight. That the castle was at the very end of the line and that it would come down to her actions tonight to save it.

She had a shallow bath, so as not to mess up her new curls, and as she washed she tried to remind herself how good-looking Bastiano was.

Even his scar did not mar his good looks.

He had been attending a wedding when they'd first met.

Maybe this time when he kissed her she would know better how to respond.

Try as she might, though, she couldn't keep her focus on Bastiano. Her thoughts strayed to Raul.

With a sob of frustration Lydia hauled herself out of the bath and dried herself.

In a last-ditch attempt, Lydia rang Arabella. Searching for an excuse—any excuse—to get out of this meeting tonight.

'Lydia!' Arabella was brusque. 'I meant to call you. You didn't say it was *this* weekend you were in Rome.'

Of course Lydia had.

'I've actually got a party on tonight,' Arabella said.

'Sounds good.'

'Invitation only.'

And of course Lydia was not invited.

And there she sat again, like a beggar beside the table, waiting for Arabella's crumbs.

'That's fine.'

Lydia rang off.

Maurice was right. She had no friends.

Arabella was her only contact from her first school, but she kept her at arm's length, and there hadn't even been a semblance of friendship at the other school.

Lydia could remember the howls of laughter from the other students when she had shaken hands and made a small curtsey for the teacher at the end of her first day.

It was what she had been taught, but of course *her* norms weren't the norms of her new school.

She didn't fit in anywhere.

Yet this morning Lydia had felt she did.

Oh, Raul had been far too forward and suggestive, but when they had spoken she had felt as if she were confiding in a friend—had felt a little as if she belonged in the world.

But all Raul wanted was sex.

Lydia had hoped for a little more.

Not a whole lot, but, yes, perhaps a little romance would be a nice side dish for her first time.

Wrong dress, Lydia thought as she looked in the mirror.

Wrong shoes, Lydia thought as she strapped on her neutral heels.

Wrong man, Lydia knew as she walked into the bar and saw Bastiano waiting.

Oh, he was terribly good-looking—even with that scar—and yet he did not move her. But perhaps *this* was romance, Lydia thought sadly, for he was charming as he ordered champagne. He was the perfect gentleman, and on the surface it was all terribly polite.

As was her life.

She thanked him for his generous hospitality. 'It's so lovely to be here. We've been looked after so well.'

'It is my pleasure,' Bastiano said. 'Are you enjoying Rome?'

'Absolutely.' Lydia smiled and thought of her far more honest response this morning with Raul.

It was after six, and she knew—just knew—that Raul wouldn't wait for very long.

And that she would regret it for ever if she missed out on tonight.

'I was thinking,' Bastiano said, 'that for dinner we might—'

'Actually…' Maurice interrupted, and put his fingers to his temples.

Lydia knew he was going to plead a headache and excuse himself from dinner. Leaving her alone with Bastiano.

It was seven minutes past six and she made her choice.

'Oh, didn't Maurice tell you?' Lydia spoke over Maurice, before he could make his excuses and leave.

Out of the corner of her eye she saw Maurice clench the glass he was holding, and she could feel his eyes shoot a stern warning, and yet Lydia spoke on.

'I'm catching up with a friend tonight—we're heading off to dinner soon. I wanted to stop by and say thank you, though.' She gave Bastiano her best false smile, but it wasn't returned. 'I don't want to get in the way of your business talk.'

'I don't think you could ever be in the way.' Bastiano's response was smooth.

'Oh, you're far too polite!' Lydia offered a small laugh to a less than impressed audience.

It sank like a stone.

'I'll leave you two to talk castles.'

She placed her unfinished drink on the table and said her farewells, and simply ignored the fury in Maurice's eyes and the muscle flickering in Bastiano's scarred cheek.

Oh, there would be consequences, Lydia knew.

But she was prepared to bear them.

For now she was free.

She wanted the red dress and the lipstick to match. She had, Lydia acknowledged, bought them for this moment, after all.

But there just wasn't time.

He could be gone already, Lydia thought in mild panic as she swept out through the revolving door.

When she glanced across the street she felt the crush of disappointment when she saw that Raul wasn't there.

But then she heard him.

'You're late.'

Lydia turned and there he was, tie loosened, tall and gorgeous, and, yes, she had made her choice.

'For the first time in my life.'

He was going to kiss her, she was sure, but she walked on ahead.

'Come on,' Lydia said quickly, worried that Maurice might follow her out.

They walked briskly, or rather Lydia did, for his stride beside her seemed slow and more measured. She felt fuelled by elation as they turned into a side street.

'Where to now?' Raul asked, and they stopped walking and she turned.

'You're the expert.'

Oh, he was—because somehow she was back against the wall with his hands on either side of her head.

She put her hands up to his chest and felt him solid beneath her palms, just felt him there for a moment, and then she looked up to his eyes.

His mouth moved in close, and as it did so she stared deeper.

She could feel heat hovering between their mouths in a slow tease before they met.

Then they met.

And all that had been missing was suddenly there.

The gentle pressure his mouth exerted, though blissful, caused a mire of sensations—until the gentleness was no longer enough.

Even before the thought was formed, he delivered.

His mouth moved more insistently and seemed to stir her from within.

Raul wanted her tongue, and yet he did not prise—he never forced a door open.

No need to.

There it was.

A slight inhalation, a hitch in her breath, and her lips parted just a little and he slipped his tongue in.

The moan she made went straight to his groin.

At first taste she was his and he knew it, for her hands moved to the back of his head, and he kissed her as hard as her fingers demanded.

More so, even.

His tongue was wicked, and her fingers tightened in his thick hair, and she could feel the wall cold and hard against her shoulders.

It was the middle of the city, just after six, and even down a side street there was no real hiding from the crowds.

Lydia didn't care.

He slid one arm around her waist to move her body away from the wall and closer to his, so that her head could fall backwards.

If there'd been a bed she would have been on it.

If there'd been a room they would have closed the door.

Yet there wasn't, and so he halted them—but only their lips.

Their bodies were heated and close and he looked her right in the eye. His mouth was wet from hers and his hair a little mussed from her fingers.

'What do you want to do?' Raul asked, knowing it was a no-brainer.

It was a very early bedtime and that suited him fine.

But the thought of waltzing her past Bastiano and Maurice no longer appealed.

A side entrance, perhaps, Raul thought, and went for her neck.

She had never thought that a kiss beneath her ear could make it impossible to breathe, let alone think.

'What do you want to do?' he whispered to her skin, and then blew on her neck, damp from his kisses. He raised his head and met her eye. 'Tonight I can give you anything you want.'

'Anything?' Lydia checked.

'Oh, yes.'

And if he was offering perfection, then she would take it.

'I want to see Rome at night—with you.'

'It's not dark yet.'

He could suggest a guided tour of his body—a very luxurious one, of course—but then he looked into her china-blue eyes.

'I want some romance with my one-night stand.'

'But I don't *do* romance.'

'Try it,' Lydia said. She didn't want some bauble in the morning and so she named her price. 'For one night.'

And Raul, who was usually *very* open to experiments, found himself reluctant to try.

Yet he had cancelled his flight for this.

And she had had the most terrible time here on her last visit, Raul knew.

The bed would always be there.

And he *had* invited her to state her wants.

He had known from the start that Lydia would make him work for his reward.

'I know just the place to start,' Raul said. 'While it's still light.'

CHAPTER FOUR

THIS WAS ROME.

He would have called for a car, but she hadn't wanted to go to the front of the hotel and risk seeing Maurice.

And so Raul found himself in his first taxi for a very long time.

He would not be repeating it!

Still, it was worth it for the result.

He took her to Aventine Hill. 'Rome's seventh hill,' he told her.

'I know that,' Lydia said. 'We came past it on a bus tour.'

'Who were you sitting with?' Raul nudged her as they walked.

'The teacher.'

'They really hated you, didn't they?'

But he put his arm around her shoulders as he said it, and it was something in the way he spoke that made her smile as she answered.

'They did.'

And then they stopped walking.

'This is the headquarters of the Order of the Knights of Malta,' he told her. 'Usually it is busy.' But tonight the stars had aligned, for there was a small group just leaving. 'Go on, then.'

'What?'

And she waited—for what, she didn't know. For him to open the door and go through?

They did neither.

'Look through the keyhole.'

Lydia bent down and did as she was told, but there was nothing to see at first—just an arch of greenery.

And then her eye grew accustomed to the view and she looked past the greenery, and there, perfectly framed in the centre, was the dome of St Peter's.

He knew the moment she saw it, for she let out a gasp.

It was a view to die for.

The soft green edging framed the eternal city and she bent there for a while, just taking it in.

It was a memory.

A magical one because it made Rome a secret garden.

Her secret garden.

By the time she stood there were others lined up, all waiting for their glimpse of heaven, and her smile told them it would be worth the wait.

Raul refused to be rushed.

'Don't you want a photo?' he asked. Assuming, of course, that she would.

'No.'

She didn't need one to remember it.

Even if Raul took her back to the hotel now, it would still be the best night ever.

In fact if Raul were to suggest taking her back to the hotel she would wave the taxi down herself, for he was kissing her again—a nice one, a not-going-anywhere one, just sharing in her excitement.

He did not take her back yet.

They walked down the hill, just talking, and he showed her the tiny streets she would never have found. He took her past the Bocca della Verità sculpture—the Mouth of Truth—though he did not tell her the legend that the old man would bite off the hand of liars.

For perhaps she might test him.

Though Raul told himself he did not lie.

He just omitted certain information.

And he continued to do so, even when the opportunity arose to reveal it.

They were now sitting on a balcony, looking out to the Colosseum, and a waiter placed their drinks down on the table.

Cognac for Raul and a cocktail that was the same fiery orange as the sky for Lydia.

He didn't assume champagne, as Bastiano had.

Like this morning at breakfast, she let her eyes wander through the menu selections.

She chose hers—he knew his.

Raul gave her choice at every turn, and that was something terribly new to Lydia.

Finally she had good memories of Rome.

'*Salute,*' Raul said, and they clinked glasses.

Wonderful memories, really.

It wasn't the sight of the Colosseum that brought a lump to her throat but the fact that *now* there were candles and flowers on the table, and that at every turn Raul had surprised her with his ease and enjoyment.

He did not sulk, nor reluctantly trudge along and put up with things before taking her to bed.

Raul led.

But she must remember it could never—for her—be the City of Love.

Raul didn't do love.

'How did Bastiano take your leaving?' Raul asked, and his question caught her by surprise, for her mind had long moved on from the hotel.

Raul himself had only just remembered the real reason he was there.

'He was fine,' Lydia replied. 'Well, he was polite. I can't blame him for being fed up—anyone would be, stuck with Maurice for the night.'

He was about to say that he doubted Bastiano would hang around anywhere he didn't choose to be, but stopped himself.

For the first time since they had met Lydia looked truly relaxed. The conversation flowed easily, and quite simply he did not want to take the chance of ruining a very nice night.

But he did need to know more. And he did not need to delve, for a very at ease Lydia was now talking.

'I know he can't stand Maurice.'

'How do you know that?'

'Because Bastiano told me.'

She was stirring her drink and didn't see the sudden tension in his features. It dawned on Raul that Bastiano and Lydia might already be lovers for all he knew.

'There was a wedding at the castle one weekend,' Lydia explained. 'It was a very good one. Of course Maurice had been through the guest list, and he made a bit of a beeline for Bastiano. He'd found out that he'd converted an old convent into a retreat, and Maurice wanted to hear his thoughts on doing something similar with the castle.'

Raul gave a disparaging laugh, and Lydia assumed it was in reference to Maurice's gall at approaching a guest.

But Raul was mocking Maurice's ignorance—Bastiano would never part with his knowledge for free.

'Bastiano wasn't interested,' Lydia said.

'Maurice told you that?' Raul checked.

'No, Bastiano did.' Lydia gave a soft laugh and looked out onto the street as she recalled that night. 'I was serving drinks, and Bastiano made some comment about saving him from the most boring man... I laughed. I knew exactly who he was referring to. But then I felt guilty, as if I ought to defend my family, and so I told him that Maurice was my stepfather.'

And there was the difference between them. Raul felt no guilt in not admitting the truth.

Perhaps a slight niggle, but he easily pushed that aside.

'You told Bastiano that Maurice was your stepfather?' he asked.

'Yes.' Lydia nodded. 'Bastiano apologised and said he would speak with him again and pay attention this time.

'And that was it?' Raul checked.

'Sorry?' Lydia frowned.

'That was all that happened between you two?'

She went pink.

'Excuse me,' Raul said. 'That is none of my business.'

The thought, though, did not sit well with him.

But then she told him.

'Just a kiss.'

She screwed up her nose as Raul breathed out in relief that they had never been lovers.

Then the relief dissolved and he loathed the fact that they had even shared a kiss.

'Come on,' he said, confused by the jealousy that arose in him. 'It's dark now.'

Oh, it was.

And busy and noisy.

It was everything Rome should be.

The Trevi Fountain had kept its promise, because she had made a wish to be back under better circumstances and now she was.

They walked for miles, and though the cobbled streets weren't stiletto-friendly Lydia felt as if she were wearing ballet slippers—the world felt lighter tonight.

'Where are we now?' Lydia asked.

'Citta Universitaria—my home for four years.'

'I would have loved to have gone to university,' Lydia said. 'I wanted to study history.'

'Why didn't you?'

'I failed my exams.'

Another truth she rarely told.

She hadn't decided to go straight into the family business, as her mother often said.

Lydia had failed all her exams.

Spectacularly.

'I messed up,' Lydia admitted.

She offered no reason or excuse although there were so many.

He knew that.

'I had to repeat some subjects after my mother died,' Raul told her. He rarely revealed anything, and certainly not his failings, yet it seemed right to do so now. 'I hit the clubs for a while.'

His honesty elicited both a smile and an admission. 'I wish that I had.'

'I moved here from Sicily to study under great protest—my father wanted me to work for him. Filthy money,' he added. 'Anyway, after my mother died for a while I made it my mission to find out how wild Rome could be at night.'

'Where in Si—'

'I lived there,' he said, pointing across the street.

She had been about to ask whereabouts in Sicily, Raul knew, but she had mentioned the convent a couple of times and perhaps knew its location. Certainly he didn't want her knowing that he and Bastiano were from the same place. So he interrupted her and gave more information about himself than he usually would.

Raul pointed upwards and Lydia found herself looking at a hotel. It was far smaller than the one they were staying at, but it was beautifully lit and from the smart cars pulling up and the guests spilling out it seemed rather exclusive.

'How could a student afford to stay in that hotel?' Lydia asked.

'It was flats back then. In fact they were very seedy.'

'And then the developers came along?'

'That was me.'

And she stared at a hotel—in the centre of Rome, for goodness' sake—and found out that he owned it. 'How?'

But Raul did not want to revisit those times.

'Come on…'

It was late—after midnight—and he'd had enough of taxis to last a lifetime, and so, despite the hour, he texted Allegra and very soon a vehicle appeared.

It wasn't a taxi!

She sat in the back and he climbed in and sat so he faced her.

It was bliss to sink into the seats. 'My feet are killing me,' Lydia admitted. 'These shoes really weren't made for walking.'

'Take them off, then,' Raul said, and he leant over and lifted her foot and placed it in his lap.

Lydia could feel his solid thigh beneath her calf, and though she willed herself to relax her leg was trembling as he started to undo the strap.

He ran his hand along her calf and found the muscle was a knot of tension. He worked it with deft fingers.

The muscle did not relax.

In fact it tightened.

And when her toes curled to his touch he placed her foot so that she could feel his desire for her.

She ought to tell him she was a virgin.

But she rather guessed that Raul wouldn't find her innocence endearing.

His fingers continued to work on the tense muscle till it loosened. High in her thigh she contracted, and then he removed the sandal and lifted her naked foot.

'Please don't,' she choked as he lifted it towards his mouth. 'I've been walking…'

'Dirty girl.'

He kissed the arch of her foot, and she tried again to pull away, but only because the wicked sensation his tongue delivered shot straight between her legs.

'Raul…' She pronounced it correctly for the first time—it simply rolled off her tongue. 'Someone might see.'

'They can't see in.'

She could see, though.

For that moment Lydia felt as if she could see inside herself.

And she was…

The feeling was so unfamiliar it took a second for Lydia to recognise just what it was.

She was happy.

Just that.

'We're here,' Raul said, and released her foot, and that tiny glimpse of carefree happiness was over.

Just like that.

For she saw him—Maurice—standing outside the hotel.

He was smoking a cigar and on his phone—no doubt to her mother.

'We'll use the side entrance.'

Raul went to the intercom to inform the driver, but her hand stopped him.

'No.'

It was over.

The windows were dark and she knew that Maurice couldn't see in—neither would he be expecting her to return in such a luxurious vehicle.

'I need to face things.'

'Tomorrow,' Raul said.

And she looked at this man who chose not to get close enough to anyone to remember a birthday.

A man who did not live by the rules.

She did.

'I think it would be better dealt with tonight. It might be a little more difficult to take the moral high road about Bastiano with my knickers in my purse.'

'Lydia…' Raul started, but then halted. He had no qualms over a one-night stand, but he conceded with a nod that she made a valid point.

'Go and tell him to get the hell out of your life, and then come to my suite.' He gave her the floor and the number, while knowing the night *he* had planned was gone. 'Will you be okay?'

'Of course I will.' Lydia gave a scoffing laugh. 'I'm twenty-four—he can hardly put me on curfew.'

'Will you be okay?' Raul asked again.

'Yes.' Lydia nodded. 'This needs to be dealt with.'

It did.

He asked his driver to move a little way down the street, and in that space of time Raul did something he rarely did. He took out a card.

Not the one he generally gave out.

'This is my number—you'll get straight through to me. If there is any problem…'

'There won't be,' Lydia said, but he opened her purse and put in the card.

This was it—both knew.

Though both hoped otherwise.

'Remember what I told you this morning,' Raul said, and she nodded.

He went to kiss her, but she moved her head to the

side. It really wasn't a turn-on, knowing that Maurice waited.

And she should never have let Raul take her shoe off, because now there was all the hassle of getting it back on.

And happiness seemed determined to elude her as she climbed out of the vehicle.

'Where the hell have you been?' Maurice asked as she approached.

'Out,' Lydia snapped.

'Your mother is worried sick,' Maurice said as they walked briskly through the foyer, though he waited until they were in the elevator to say any more. 'I'm trying to save *your* family's business and you walk out on the one person who could help do just that.'

'I came for a drink.'

'He wanted to take us both to dinner. I've said to Bastiano that you'll be there tomorrow.'

'Well, you shouldn't have,' Lydia retorted.

They got out of the elevator and Lydia headed for her suite. 'I'm going to bed.'

'Don't you walk away from me,' Maurice told her. 'You'll be there tomorrow night, with a smile on, and—'

'Maurice, *why* do I need to be there?' She pointed out what Raul had this morning. 'I don't hold the deeds to the castle—my mother does. And I don't actually *like* the idea of turning it into a retreat. There's absolutely no reason for me to be there.'

'You know there is.'

'But *why*?'

Say it, Maurice, Lydia thought. *Have the guts to voice it out loud.*

'Because Bastiano wants you.'

'Then you need to tell him that I'm not part of the deal.' Her voice was shaky. The truth, even if deep down she'd already known it, was actually very difficult to hear said out loud. 'In fact you can tell Bastiano that, as of now, I no longer live or work at the castle.'

'Lydia, he's a charming man, he's extremely wealthy, and he's very interested in you.'

'Well, I'm not for sale! I've told you—I'm leaving.'

'And where are you going to go? Lydia, you've got no qualifications, no savings...'

'Odd, that,' Lydia responded, 'when I've been living at home and working my backside off for the last six years.'

She was done, she was through, and she dug in her purse for her keycard and let herself into her suite.

Maurice knocked loudly.

Oh, my God.

She could not take even another night of this.

She didn't have to, Lydia realised as she recalled Raul's advice.

'You can walk away from anyone you choose to and you don't have to come up with a reason.'

She had *many* good reasons to walk, Lydia thought, and started throwing her possessions into her case.

'Your mother is going to be very upset...' Maurice called through the door, but he fell silent when it was opened and Lydia stood holding her case.

'I'm leaving.'

'What the hell...? Lydia...'

Lydia could see a bit of spittle at the side of his mouth, and she could feel his anger at her refusal to comply.

When she always had in the past.

For the sake of her mother Lydia would generally back down when things got heated—but for the sake of herself she now stood her ground.

It was as if the blinkers had been lifted, and she could now see the control and the pressure he exerted.

And she would play the game no more.

No, she could not save the castle and, no, she would not meekly comply just to keep his mood tolerable. She could almost feel the eggshells she had walked on dissolving beneath her feet.

She marched to the elevators and he followed. He reached for her as she reached the doors and suddenly she was scared.

Raul had been right to be concerned.

She *was* scared of Maurice and his temper.

Oh, she wasn't running to Raul—she was running away from hell.

Maurice slapped her.

He delivered a stinging slap to her cheek and pulled at her hair, raised his other hand—but somehow she freed herself.

Lydia ducked into the elevator and wrenched the doors closed on his hand.

'Thank you,' she said. With the gate safely between them she spoke in a withering tone. 'Now I know for a fact what an utter bastard you are.'

She did not crumple.

Lydia refused to.

And she refused to waste even a single tear.

She was scared, though.

Scared and alone.

And she would have run into the night.

Without Raul, absolutely she would have run.

But instead of going down Lydia pressed the elevator button that would take her to his floor.

CHAPTER FIVE

RAUL STEPPED INTO his suite, unexpectedly alone.

Allegra had, of course, rung ahead, and everything had been prepared for Raul to return with a female guest.

The suite was dimly lit, but Raul saw champagne chilling in a bucket. He bypassed it. Throwing his jacket on a chair, he poured a large cognac and downed half in one gulp, then kicked off his socks and shoes, wrenched off his tie and removed his shirt.

In the bathroom Raul rolled his eyes, for the sight that greeted him seemed to mock. Candles had been lit and the deep bath was filled with fragrant water. But Raul would be bypassing that too—perhaps a cold shower might be more fitting.

He soon gave up prowling the penthouse suite dressed for two and lay on the bed. He took another belt of his drink and considered extending his stay for another night in Rome.

Unlike before, when he had actually wanted to flaunt Lydia under Bastiano's nose, Raul suddenly had a sense of foreboding.

Yes, Lydia might have stood up to her stepfather tonight, but for how long would that last? She was strong—Raul had seen that—but her family clearly saw Lydia as their ticket out of whatever mess they were in. And Bastiano, Raul knew, didn't care *what* methods he used to get his own way.

It wasn't his problem.

Over and over Raul told himself that.

He was angry with Bastiano rather than concerned about Lydia, Raul decided.

Only that didn't sit quite right.

Tomorrow he would be out of here.

Raul had rescheduled the jet for midday tomorrow. He would soon be back in Venice and this trip would be forgotten.

Raul didn't even want the hotel now—Sultan Alim's words had hit home. The Grande Lucia was far too much responsibility. He wanted investments he could manage from a distance. Raul wanted no labour of love.

In any area of his life.

Raul managed to convince himself that he was relieved with tonight's outcome.

Well, not relieved.

Far from it.

He was aching and hard, and was just sliding down his zipper, when he heard knocking at the door.

Good things, Raul realised as he made his way to the door, did come to those who waited. For just when he had thought the night was over, it would seem it had just begun!

He didn't bother to turn on the lounge light—just opened the door and Lydia tumbled in.

She had a suitcase beside her, which would usually be enough to perturb him, but there were other concerns right now.

She was shaking while trying to appear calm.

'Sorry to disturb you…'

Her voice was trembling.

'What happened?'

'We had a row,' Lydia said. 'A long overdue one. Anyway, I don't want to talk about that now.'

Oh, it wasn't just that she knew the price for a night in his room—Lydia wanted to go back to feeling happy.

Preferably now, please.

She wanted the oblivion his mouth offered, not to think of the turbulent times ahead.

He was naked from the waist up and her demand was sudden. 'Where were we?'

And her mouth found his and her kiss was urgent.

He tasted of liquor, and he was obviously aroused when she pressed into him.

Yet for once Raul was the one slowing things down.

His body demanded he kiss her back with fervour, that he take her now, up against the wall, and give her what she craved.

Yet there was more to this, he knew.

'Lydia…'

He peeled her off him and it was a feat indeed, for between his attempts to halt her he was resisting going back in for a kiss. He was hard and primed, and she was desperate and willing.

An obvious match.

Yet somehow not.

'Slow down…' he told her. 'Angry sex we can do later.'

Raul never thought of 'later' with women and was

surprised by his own thought process, but his over-riding feeling was concern.

'I'm not angry,' Lydia said.

She could feel his arms holding her back as he somehow read her exactly and told her how she felt.

'Oh, baby, you are!'

She was.

Lydia was a ball of fury that he held at arm's length.

She was trying to go for his zipper. She was actually wild.

'Lydia?'

He guided her to a chair, and it was like folding wood trying to get her to sit down, but finally he did.

Lydia could hear her own rapid breathing as Raul went over and flicked on a light, and she knew he was right.

She was angry.

He saw her pale face and the red hand mark, and Raul's own anger coiled his gut tight. But he kept his voice even. 'What happened?'

'I told Maurice that I shan't be his puppet and neither shall I be returning home.'

He came to her and knelt down, and his hand went to her swollen cheek.

'Did he hit you anywhere else?'

'No.' She shook her head. 'I'm fine. Really I am.'

Raul frowned, because there were no tears—it was suppressed rage that glittered in her eyes.

'Do you want me to go and sort him out?'

'I would hate that.'

He rather guessed that she would.

'Please?' he said, and saw that she gave a small smile.

'No.'

He would do so later.

Right now, though, Raul's concern was Lydia. He stood and looked around. There was a woman in his hotel suite, and for the first time Raul didn't know what to do with her.

Lydia too looked around, and she was starting to calm.

She saw the champagne and the flowers, and the room that had been prepared for them, and cringed at her own behaviour. She had asked for romance and he had delivered, and then she'd thrust herself on him.

'Can we pretend the last fifteen minutes never happened?' Lydia asked.

'You want me to go back to licking your feet?'

Lydia laughed.

Not a lot, but on a night when laughter should be an impossible task somehow she did.

She felt calmer.

Though she was shaken, and embarrassed at foisting herself upon Raul, now that she had stood up to Maurice she felt clearer in the head than she had in years.

'Do you want a drink?'

She nodded.

'What would you like?'

And she could see his amber drink and still taste it on her tongue.

'The same as you.'

'So, what happened?' Raul asked, and she answered as he crossed the suite.

'A necessary confrontation, and one that's been a

long time coming,' she admitted. 'I've hated him since the day my mother first brought him home.'

'How long after your father died?'

'Eighteen months. Maurice had all these lavish ideas for the castle—decided to use it for weddings.'

'I hate weddings,' Raul said, taking the stopper off the bottle and pouring her a drink. 'Imagine having to deal with one every week.'

'They're not every week—unfortunately. Sometimes in the summer...' Her voice trailed off midsentence and Raul knew why. He was minus his shirt, and with his back to her, therefore Lydia must have seen his scar.

She had.

It was the sort of scar that at first glance could stop a conversation.

A jagged fault line on a perfect landscape, for he was muscled and defined, but then she frowned as she focused on the thinner lines.

A not so perfect landscape.

Oh, so badly she wanted to know more about this man.

But Lydia remembered her manners and cleared her throat and resumed talking.

'In the summer they used to be weekly, but the numbers have been dwindling.'

'Why?' Raul asked, and handed her the drink. He was grateful that she had said nothing about the scars. He loathed it when women asked about them, as if one night with him meant access to his past.

And it was always just one night.

Lydia took a sip. In truth it had tasted better on his tongue, but it was warming and pleasant and she focused on that for a moment. But then Raul asked the question again.

'Why are the numbers dwindling?'

'Because when people book a luxury venue they expect luxury at every turn, but Maurice cuts corners.'

He had heard that so many times.

In fact Raul had made his fortune from just that. He generally bought hotels on their last legs and turned them into palaces.

The Grande Lucia was a different venture—this hotel was a palace already, and that was why he was no longer considering making the purchase.

'Maurice is always after the quick fix,' Lydia said, and then stilled when she heard the buzzing of her phone.

'It's him,' Lydia said.

'I'll speak to him for you,' Raul said, and went to pick it up.

'Please don't.' Her voice was very clear. 'You would only make things worse.'

'How?'

'You won't be the one dealing with the fallout.'

And, yes, he *could* deal with Maurice tonight, but who would that really help? Oh, it might make Raul feel better, and Maurice certainly deserved it, but Lydia was right—it wouldn't actually help things in the long run, given he wouldn't be around.

'Turn your phone off,' Raul suggested, but she shook her head.

'I can't—he'll call my mother and she'll be worried.'

Raul wasn't so sure about that. He rather guessed

that Lydia's mother would more likely be annoyed that Lydia hadn't meekly gone along with their plans.

He watched as her phone rang again, but when she looked at it this time, instead of being angry she screwed her eyes closed.

'Maurice?'

'No, it's my mother.'

'Ignore it.'

'I can't,' Lydia said. 'He must have told her I've run off.' Her phone fell silent, but Lydia knew it wouldn't stay like that for very long. 'I'll ring her and tell her I'm safe. I shan't tell her where I am—just that I'm fine. Can I...?' She gestured to the double doors and it was clear that Lydia wanted some privacy to make the call.

'Of course.'

It was a bedroom.

Her first time in a man's bedroom, and it was so far from the circumstances she had hoped for that it was almost laughable.

It had been an almost perfect night, yet it was ruined now. Lydia sat on the bed and cringed as she recalled her entrance into his suite.

Lydia was very used to hiding her true feelings, yet Raul seemed to bring them bubbling up to the surface.

Right now, though, she needed somehow to snap back to efficient mode—though it was hard when she heard her mother's accusatory voice.

'What the hell are you playing at, Lydia?'

'I'm not playing at anything.'

'You know damn well how important this trip is!'

A part of Lydia had hoped for her mother to take her side. To agree that Maurice's behaviour tonight had been preposterous and tell her that of *course* Lydia didn't have to agree to anything she didn't want to do.

It had been foolish to hope.

Instead Lydia sat there as her mother told her how charming Bastiano was, how he'd been nothing but a gentleman to date, and asked how she dared embarrass the family like this.

And then, finally, her mother was honest.

'It's time you stepped up...'

'Bastiano doesn't even know me,' Lydia pointed out. 'We've spoken, at best, a couple of times.'

'Lydia, it's time to get your head out of the clouds. I've done everything I can to keep us from going under. For whatever reason, Bastiano has taken an interest in you...'

Lydia didn't hear much of the rest.

For whatever reason...

As if it was unfathomable that someone might simply want her for no other reason than they simply did.

It was Lydia who ended the call, and after sitting for a few minutes in silence she looked up when there was a knock at the door.

'Come in,' Lydia said, and then gave a wry smile as Raul entered—it was *his* bedroom, after all.

'How did it go with your mother?'

'Not very well,' Lydia admitted. 'I'm being overly dramatic, apparently.'

'Why don't you have a bath?'

'A bath!' A laugh shot out of her pale lips at his odd suggestion.

'It might relax you. There's one already run.'

'I'm guessing I wouldn't have been bathing alone, had I come up the first time.'

'Plans change,' Raul said. 'Give me your phone and go and wind down.'

'You won't answer it?' Lydia checked.

'No,' Raul said.

Her family was persistent.

Raul, though, was stubborn.

The phone continued to buzz, but rather than turn it off Raul went back to lying on the bed, as he had been when Lydia had arrived.

And that was how she found him.

The bath *had* been soothing. Lydia had lain in the fragrant water, terribly glad of his suggestion to leave her phone.

It had given her a chance to calm down and to regroup.

'They've been calling,' Raul told her by way of greeting.

'I thought that they might.' Lydia sighed. 'I doubt they'll give up if Bastiano hasn't. Apparently Maurice has said he'll meet him tomorrow and I'm supposed to be there.'

'And what did you say?'

'No, of course—but it's not just about dinner with Bastiano…'

'Of course it's not,' Raul agreed.

'I think he wants sex.'

'He wants more than sex, Lydia. He wants to marry you. He thinks you'd make a very nice trophy wife. Bastiano wants to be King of your castle.'

He watched for her reaction and as always she surprised him, because Lydia just gave a shrug.

'I wouldn't be the first to marry for money.'

And though the thought appalled her it did not surprise her.

'I doubt my mother married Maurice for his sparkling personality,' Lydia said, and Raul gave a small nod that told her he agreed. 'Would *you* marry for money?' Lydia asked.

'No,' Raul said, 'but that's not from any moral standpoint—I just would never marry.'

'Why?'

'I've generally run out of conversation by the morning. I can't imagine keeping one going with the same person for the rest of my life.'

He did make her smile.

And he put her at ease.

No, that wasn't the word, because *ease* wasn't what she felt around him.

She felt like herself.

Whoever that was.

Lydia had never really been allowed to find out.

'You'd have to remember her birthday,' Lydia said, and sat next to him when he patted the bed.

'And our anniversary.' Raul rolled his eyes. 'And married people become obsessed with what's for dinner.'

'They do!' Lydia agreed.

'I had a perfectly normal PA—Allegra. Now, every day, her husband rings and they talk about what they are going to have for dinner. I pay her more than enough that she could eat out every night...'

Yes, he made her smile.

'Do you believe in love?' Lydia asked.

'No.'

She actually liked how abruptly he dismissed the very notion.

It was so peaceful in his room, and though common sense told her she should be nervous Lydia wasn't. It was nice to talk with someone who was so matter-of-fact about something she had wrestled with for so long.

'Would you marry if it meant you might save your family from going under?'

'My family is gone.' Raul shrugged. 'Anyway, you can't save anyone from going under. Whatever you try and do.'

The sudden pensive note to his voice had her turning to face him.

'I wanted my mother to leave my father. I did everything I could to get her to leave, but she wouldn't. I knew I had to get out. I was working a part-time job in Rome and studying, and I had found a flat for her.' He looked over at Lydia briefly. 'Next to the one I told you about. But she wouldn't leave. She said that she could not afford to, and that aside from that she took her wedding vows seriously.'

'I would too,' Lydia told him.

'Well, my mother said the same—but then she had an affair.' It was surprisingly easy to tell her, given what Lydia had shared with him. 'She died in a car accident just after the affair was exposed. I doubt her mind was on the road. After she died I found out that she'd had access to more than enough money to start a new life. I think her lover had found that out too.'

He wanted to tell her that his mother's lover had been Bastiano, but that wasn't the point he was trying to make, and he did not want to make things worse for her tonight.

'Lydia, what I'm trying to say is you can't prevent anyone from going under.'

'I don't believe that.'

'Even if you marry him, do you really think Bastiano is going to take advice from Maurice? Do you think he will want to keep your mother and her husband in residence?'

He took out all her dark thoughts, the fears that had kept her awake at night, and forced her to examine them.

'No.'

'Take it from me—the only person you can ever save is yourself.'

Strong words, but clearly she didn't take them in, because when her phone buzzed Lydia went to pick it up.

'Leave it,' Raul said.

'I can't do that,' Lydia admitted. 'I might turn it off.'

'Then they'll know you're avoiding them. Just ignore it.'

'I can't.'

'Yes, you can—because I shan't let you hear it.'

She had thought Raul meant he would turn the ring down, but instead as the phone started to ring again he reached for her and drew her face towards him.

Nothing, Lydia was sure, could take her mind from her family tonight.

She was wrong.

His kiss was softer than the others he had delivered. So light, in fact, that as she closed her eyes in anticipation all he gave was a light graze to her lips that had her hungry for more as his hand slid into her hair.

Kiss by soft kiss he took care of every pin, and Lydia found her lips had parted, but still he made her wait for his tongue.

She had tasted him already, and her body was hungry for more.

Yet he was cruel in attack for he gave so little.

He undid the knot of her robe with the same measured pace he had taken in dealing with her hair and then pushed it down over her arms so that she sat naked.

Lydia felt something akin to panic as contact ceased and he ran his gaze down her body. It *wasn't* panic, though, she thought. It was far nicer—because as the phone buzzed by the bed she was staring down at him, watching his mouth near her breast, and she would have died rather than answer it.

'Do you want to get that?' Raul asked, and she could feel his breath on her breast.

'No...' Her voice had gone—it came out like a husk.

'I can't hear you,' he said, and then he delivered his tongue in a motion too light, for she bunched the sheet with her fingers and fought not to grab his head.

'No,' she said, and when his mouth paused in delivering its magic, she added, 'I don't want to answer.'

'Good.'

He sucked hard now, and she knew he bruised.

Raul gave one breast the deep attention that her mouth had craved, and she fought not to swear or, worse, to plead.

She should tell him that he was her first, Lydia

thought as he guided her hand to his crotch and she felt his thick, hard length through the fabric.

But then her phone buzzed again and the teasing resumed, for he stood.

'Do you want me to get that?'

'Turn it off,' Lydia said.

'Oh, no.'

He slid down his zipper and the buzz of the phone dimmed in her ears when she saw him naked.

Yes, that would hurt.

Oh, she really should tell him, Lydia thought as she reached out to hold him. But then she closed her eyes at the bliss of energy beneath her fingers and the low moan that came from him as his hand closed around hers.

He moved her slender fingers more roughly than she would have. She opened her eyes at the feel of him.

She could hear their breathing, rapid and shallow, and then his free hand took her head and pushed it down, and she tasted him just a little as her tongue caressed him.

And for Raul, what should have been too slow, the touch of her tongue too light, somehow she owned the night.

The slight choking in her throat closing around him brought him close to release, so that he was grateful for the sudden buzzing and it was Raul who was briefly distracted.

Lydia wasn't.

She was lost in the taste of him when for the second time that night—but for a very different reason—she felt a tug on her hair and looked up.

Now when she licked her lips it was to savour the taste of him.

And Raul, who did not want this to be over, put her to bed.

On top of it.

Raul was decisive in his positioning of Lydia, and her loose limbs were his to place.

He knelt astride her and put her arms above her head, held them one-handed as the other hand played with the breast he wasn't sucking.

'Raul…' She was about to tell him about her virginal status, but her phone buzzed again and he thought that was her complaint.

'Shush…'

And then he moved so that he knelt between her legs, and reached to the bedside drawer for a condom, and she lay there watching as he rolled it on.

'Raul…' Her voice was breathless, but she should say it now—she was trying to.

'You talk too much.'

She had said two words and both had been his name. She went to point that out but lost her thought processes as his head went down between her legs and she lay holding her breath and nervously awaiting his intimate touch.

He kissed her exactly as he had the first time.

Raul's mouth lightly pressed *there*, and then there was the tease of his tongue. Slowly at first, as Lydia had been slow, for he thought she had been teasing him at the time.

'Please…' Lydia said, not sure if she was asking to speak, asking him to slow down or asking for more.

His jaw was rough, his mouth soft and his tongue probing. It was sublime.

His mouth worked on and she started to moan.

His tongue urged her on.

Lydia's thighs were shaking and she fought to stay silent. And then she gave in, and he moaned in pleasure as she orgasmed. He kissed her and swallowed as she pulsed against his lips.

And then he left them.

She was heated and twitching, breathless and giddy and perfectly done as he moved over her and crushed her tense lips with his moist ones. His thigh moved between her legs and splayed her, and even coming down from a high, with the feel of him nudging and the energy of him, Lydia knew this would hurt.

'Slowly,' she said, but her words were muffled, so she turned her head. 'I've never—'

He was about to aim for hard, fast and deep, when he heard those two words that were so unexpected.

'Slowly,' she said again.

He could do that.

An unseen smile stretched his lips at the thought of taking her first, practically beneath Bastiano's nose. And then the thought of taking her first made his ardour grow.

But then, just when bliss appeared on the menu, the stars seemed to collect and become one that shone too bright. And, like a headmaster grabbing an errant student by the shoulder, he suddenly hauled himself back from the edge.

Everything went still.

All the delicious sensations, gathering tight, slowly

loosened as his weight came down on her rather than within her.

And then he rolled off and onto his back and lay breathless, unsated, both turned on and angry.

He told her why. 'I don't do virgins.'

There was so much she could protest at about that statement.

Do?

And her response was tart, to cover up her disappointment and, yes, her embarrassment that he had brought things to a very shuddering halt.

'What, only experienced applicants need apply?'

'Don't you get it?' He ripped off the condom and tossed it aside, and ached to finish the job. 'There's nothing to apply *for*, Lydia. I like one-night stands. I like to get up in the morning and have coffee and then go about my day. It's sex. That's it. There are no vacant positions waiting to be filled in my life.'

'I wasn't expecting anything more.'

'You say that *now*.'

And *now* Raul sulked.

He had heard it so many times before.

Raul didn't *do* virgins, and with good reason— because even the most seasoned of his lovers tended to ask for more than he was prepared to give.

'I mean it,' Lydia insisted.

'Do you know what, Lydia? If you've waited till you're twenty-four I'm guessing there's a reason.'

There was—she'd hardly had men beating down the door.

But a small voice was telling her that Raul, as arrogant as his words were, was actually right—making love *would* change things for her.

Then again, since she had met Raul everything had already changed.

'Go to sleep,' he said.

'I can't.'

'Yes, Lydia, *you* can.'

His voice was sulky, and she didn't know what he meant, but as she lay there Lydia started to understand.

She felt a little as if she was floating.

All the events of the night were dancing before her eyes, and she could watch them unfold without feeling—except for one.

'What happened to your back?'

Her voice came from that place just before she fell asleep. Raul knew that.

Yet he wished she had not asked.

Lydia had not asked about one scar but about his whole back.

He did not want to think about that.

But now he was starting to.

CHAPTER SIX

'IT'S YOUR MOTHER'S FUNERAL,' the priest admonished,
but only once Raul had been safely cuffed and led
away.

Raul and Bastiano, the police decided, should not
be in the same building, so Raul was taken to the
jailhouse to cool down and Bastiano was cuffed to
a stretcher and taken to the valley's small hospital.

A towel covered Raul's injury, and he sat in a cell
until a doctor came to check on him.

Raul loathed anyone seeing his back, due to the
scars his father had put there, but thankfully the doctor didn't comment on them. He took one look at the
gaping wound and shook his head.

'This is too big to repair under a local,' the doctor informed him. 'I'll tell the guards to arrange your
transfer to the hospital.'

'Is Bastiano still there?' Raul asked, and the doctor nodded. 'Then you'll do it here.'

The thought of being in the same building as Bastiano tonight was not one he relished, and a hospital
was no place for his current mood.

'It's going to hurt,' the doctor warned.

But Raul already did.

The closure of the wound took ages.

He felt the fizz and sear of the peroxide as it bubbled its way through raw flesh, and then came the jab of the doctor's fingers as he explored it.

'I really think...' the doctor started, but Raul did not change his stance.

'Just close it.'

Deep catgut sutures closed the muscles and then thick silk finally drew together the skin.

He was written up for some painkillers to be taken throughout the night when required, but he did not bother to ask the guards for them.

Nothing could dim the pain.

It was not the wounds of the flesh that caused agony, more the memories and regret.

He should have known what was going on.

His mother's more cheerful disposition on his last visit was because she'd had a lover. Raul knew that now.

And there was guilt too—tangible guilt—because she had called him on the morning she had died and Raul had not picked up.

Instead he had been deep in oblivion with some no-name woman and had chosen not to take the call.

Raul lay on the hard, narrow bed and stared at the ceiling through the longest night of his life.

There would be many more to come.

Light came in through the barred windows and he heard a drunk who had sung the night through being processed and released.

And then another.

Raul was in no rush for his turn.

'Hey.'

The heavy door opened and a police officer brought him coffee. He was familiar.

Marco.

They had been at school together.

'For what it's worth, I'm on your side,' Marco told Raul as he handed him a coffee. 'Bastiano's a snake. I wish they had let you finish the job.'

Raul said nothing—just accepted the coffee.

God, but he hated the valley. There was corruption at every turn. If memory served him correctly, and it usually did, Bastiano had slept with the young woman who was now Marco's fiancée.

Just after nine Raul signed the papers for his release and Marco handed him his tie and belt, which Raul pocketed.

'Smarten up,' Marco warned him. 'You are to be at the courthouse by ten.'

Raul put on his belt and tucked in his shirt somewhat but gave up by the time he got to his tie. One look in the small washroom mirror and he knew it was pointless. His eyes were bruised purple, his lips swollen, his hair matted with blood and he needed to shave.

Groggy, his head pounding, Raul stepped out onto the street into a cruelly bright day and walked the short distance to the courthouse. Raul assumed he was there to be formally charged, but instead he found out it was for the reading of Maria Di Savo's last will and testament.

His father, Gino, was there for that, of course. And he sat gloating, because he knew that apart from the very few trinkets he had given her in earlier years everything Maria had had was his.

Raul just wanted it over and done with, and then he would get the hell out.

He was done with Casta for good.

But then, for the second time in less than twenty-four hours, the man he hated most in the world appeared— again at the most inappropriate time.

'What the hell is *he* doing here?'

It was Gino who rose in angry response as an equally battered Bastiano took a seat on a bench. His face had been sutured and a jagged scar ran the length of his now purple cheek. Clearly he had just come from the hospital, for he was still wearing yesterday's suit.

And then the judge commenced the reading of the will.

This was a mere formality, and Raul simply hoped he might get the crucifix Maria had always worn.

That wish came true, for he was handed a slim envelope and the simple cross and chain fell onto his palm.

But then out slid a ring.

It was exquisite—far more elaborate than anything his mother had owned—rose gold with an emerald stone, it was dotted with tiny seed pearls and it felt heavy in his palm. Raul picked it up between finger and thumb and tried to place it, yet he could not remember his mother wearing it.

He was distracted from examining the ring when the judge spoke again.

'Testamona Segreto.'

Even the rather bored court personnel stood to attention, as suddenly there was an unexpected turn in the formalities.

Raul stopped looking at the ring and Gino frowned and leant forward as all present learnt that his mother had made a secret will.

More intriguing was the news that it been amended just a few short weeks ago.

A considerable sum had been left to Maria on the death of her brother, Luigi, on condition that it did not in any way benefit Maria's husband.

Luigi had loathed Gino.

But Luigi had died some ten years ago.

Most shocking for Raul was the realisation that his mother had had the means to leave.

Raul had been working his butt off, trying to save to provide for her, when she could have walked away at any time.

It made no sense.

Nothing in his life made sense any more.

And then Raul felt a pulse beat a tattoo in his temples as the judge read out his mother's directions.

'The sum is to be divided equally between my son Raul Di Savo and Bastiano Conti. My hope is that they use it wisely. My prayer is that they have a wonderful life.'

Raul sat silent as pandemonium broke out in the courthouse. Money was Gino's god, and *this* betrayal hit harder than the other. He started cursing, and as he moved to finish off Raul's work on Bastiano, Security were called.

'He gets nothing!' Gino sneered, and jabbed his finger towards Bastiano. 'Maria was sick in the head— she would not have known what she was doing when she made that will.'

'The testimonial is clear,' the judge responded calmly as Gino was led out.

'Bastiano used her. Tell him that we will fight...' Gino roared over his shoulder.

Raul said nothing in response—just sat silent as his mother's final wishes sank in.

She had chosen Bastiano as the second benefactor and had asked that her money be divided equally...

Oh, that stung.

He looked over at Bastiano, who stared ahead and refused to meet his gaze.

Why the hell had she left it to *him*? Had Bastiano known about the money and engineered the entire thing? Had he sweet-talked her into changing her will and then deliberately exposed their affair, knowing that the fragile Maria could never survive the fallout?

Gino was still shouting from the corridor. 'I stood by her all these years!'

Raul sat thinking. He knew he could contest this in court—or he could wait till he and Bastiano were outside and fight. This time to the bloody end.

He chose the latter.

Outside, the sun seemed to chip at his skull and he felt like throwing up—and then Bastiano stepped out, also wincing at the bright afternoon sun.

'So,' Raul said by way of greeting, 'the gossip in the valley was wrong.' He watched as Bastiano's brow creased in confusion, and then he better explained. 'As it turns out—*you* were the whore.'

The court attendees spilled out onto the street, the guards hovered, and a police vehicle drove slowly past. Raul saw that Marco was at the wheel.

As it slid out of sight Raul knew that if Marco was summoned to a fight outside the courthouse the response time would be slow.

They stared at each other.

Raul's black eyes met Bastiano's silver-grey and they shared their mutual loathing.

'Your mother...' Bastiano started, and then, perhaps wisely, chose not to continue—though that did not stop Raul.

'Are you going to tell me to respect her wishes?' Raul sneered. 'You knew she had this money—you knew...' He halted, but only because his voice was close to faltering and he would not allow Bastiano to glimpse weakness.

He would beat Bastiano with more than his fists.

Raul cleared his throat and delivered his threat, low but strong, and for Bastiano's ears only. 'Collect promptly...pay slowly.'

It was an old Italian saying, but it came with different meaning on this day.

Bastiano might have collected promptly today, but he would pay.

And slowly.

Their eyes met, and though nothing further was said it was as if Raul had repeated those words and he watched as his threat sank in.

Raul would keep his word—the vow he had made by his mother's grave.

Every day he would fight Bastiano—not with fists but with action, and so, to the chagrin of the gathered crowd, who wanted the day to end in blood, Raul walked away.

Bastiano might have got a payout today, but Raul

would take his mother's inheritance and build a life from it far away from here.

And in the process he would destroy Bastiano at every opportunity.

Revenge would be his motivator now.

CHAPTER SEVEN

LYDIA KNEW EXACTLY where she was even before her eyes had opened.

There was constant awareness of him, even in sleep. Hearing his deep breathing and feeling his warm, sleeping body beside her, Lydia thought it was the nicest awakening she had ever had.

She chose not to stretch, or pull herself out of this slumberous lull. The mattress felt like a cloud, and the room was the perfect temperature, because even with the bedding around her waist she was warm.

Raul's back did not make pleasant viewing.

Oh, it was muscled, and his shoulders were wide, and his black hair narrowed neatly into the nape of his neck. All was perfect except for the scars.

And there were a lot of them.

There was the ugly, thick vertical one that was untidy and jagged and ran from mid-shoulder to waist.

But there were others that ran across his back.

Thin white lines…row upon row.

She had asked him about his back last night.

Lydia lay there trying to recall his answer.

There hadn't been one.

And she did not ask with words this time—instead

with touch, for while she had been looking at his back her fingers had inadvertently gone there.

Raul felt the question in her touch and loathed the fact that he had fallen to sleep on his side, and he rolled onto his back.

'I'm sorry I asked,' Lydia said.

'Then why did you?'

'Because when I'm with you I seem to forget to be polite.'

A phone rang, and this time it wasn't Lydia's. The battery had finally given out.

Raul reached over and swore, even before he had answered the call and then he spoke for a few minutes and lay back down—but this time he faced her.

'We overslept.'

'What time is it?'

'Midday.'

Lydia's eyes widened in surprise. 'Did you miss your plane?'

'No, it is missing me. That's why Allegra rang. She's going to reschedule.'

He stared at her and Lydia found out then why she had thrown herself at him last night.

It was the correct response to those black eyes, Lydia realised, because her desire was still the same.

'Sorry I didn't tell you I was a virgin.'

'It's a miracle you still are.'

She didn't want to be, though.

How heavenly to be made love to by him, Lydia thought, though she said not a word.

He reached out a hand and moved her hair back from her face, and still nothing was said. Lydia liked sharing this silent space with him.

No demands—just silence.

He thought again of all she'd told him—how she had sat at breakfast yesterday and given him that dark piece of her past.

And they were back in that place, together again, only this time it was Raul who spoke.

'I got into a fight at my mother's funeral. At the cemetery.'

'Oh, dear.'

She smiled—not a happy one, just a little smile at their differences.

And he gave a thin smile too.

'With whom?' Lydia asked.

'Her lover.'

And it was at that moment, when he didn't name Bastiano, that Raul, for the first time, properly lied.

Oh, last night it had technically been a lie by omission. She had been angry and confused and there had been good reason for him not to disclose. But now they were in bed together, facing each other and talking as if they were lovers, and Raul knew at his base that he should at that moment have told her.

Yet he did not want her to turn away.

Which she would.

Of course she would.

'When did you find out that your mother was having an affair?' Lydia asked.

'Right after she died,' Raul said. 'I didn't believe it at first. My mother was very religious—when she was a girl, growing up she had hoped to be a nun…'

'Why didn't she?'

'She got pregnant at sixteen.'

'With you? By your father?'

'Of course.' Raul gave a nod. 'It wasn't a happy marriage, I knew that, but I was still surprised...' He didn't finish.

'To find that she cheated?' Lydia asked, and watched his eyes narrow at her choice of words.

'I think my mother was the one who was cheated.' He thought of Bastiano's slick charm and the inheritance that he had ensured was signed over to his name.

'Or,' Lydia pondered out loud, 'maybe she fell in love.'

'Please!' Raul's voice was derisive, but more at Lydia's suggestion than at her. And then he told her something. 'She was used. I hate that man.'

'Do you ever see him?' Lydia asked. 'Her lover?'

'On occasion,' Raul admitted. 'I have made it my mission to take from him, to get there first, to beat him at everything...' It was the reason he was here at the Hotel Grande Lucia. Usually he would be ringing Allegra, drafting an offer to put to Alim.

Yet he had slept until midday.

And that need to conquer had been the real reason for pulling back last night.

Lydia deserved far better than that.

And it was there again—the chance to tell her just who Bastiano was, here and now, in bed, during the most intimate conversation of his life—for Raul never usually discussed such things.

But he didn't tell.

There was no need for that.

And anyway she would be gone soon. So Raul kissed her instead.

It was a different kiss from last night—they knew

more about each other now than then—but it did not last for long.

Raul knew his own reputation, and that it wouldn't be changing any time soon, and so he pulled back.

She was dismissed.

Yet still they lingered in bed.

'What are you going to do with the rest of your day?' he asked her.

'I'm going to head home while I've still got one. I'll see if I can transfer my flight to today,' Lydia said. 'I want to tell my mother—away from Maurice—that I'm moving out.'

'Good,' Raul said. 'You need to…' He halted. It was not his place to tell her what to do.

'I know what I need to do, Raul.'

She closed her eyes for a moment and thought of the mountain in front of her that she was about to climb—walking out on the family business, forging a career of her own, finding somewhere to live with nothing.

Yet there was excitement there too.

It was time.

And that made her smile.

'What will *you* do today?' Lydia asked.

Raul thought for a moment—the weekend spread out before him, and really he could take his pick.

Allegra was waiting for Raul to call with his amended schedule.

There were parties and invitations galore—particularly as he was known to be in Rome. And yet whatever he chose Raul knew it could not top last night.

'I'll go home,' Raul said.

'And where's that?' Lydia asked.

'Venezia.'

Venice.

Lydia gave a wistful sigh, but then, so contrary were her memories from there, she screwed up her nose just a fraction—and he saw that she did.

To cover herself, and because she could not take him delving deep this morning, she quickly chose laughter and gave him a dig in his ribs.

'You never told me that you lived there.'

'Why would I?'

'When I was talking about it you never let on...' And then she halted, remembering that Raul owed her no explanations—they danced on the edge of the other, revealing only what they chose. 'I'm not very good at being a one-night stand.'

'No,' he agreed with a wry smile, 'you're not.' And then his smile dimmed, but still his eyes held hers and Raul asked a question. 'Would you have regretted it if we had slept together?'

'No.' Lydia shook her head. 'Raul, you seem to have decided that just because I haven't slept with anyone I'm looking for something permanent. By all accounts I could have had that with Bastiano, but I chose not to. He's not...' Lydia faltered and then, rather than finishing, swallowed her words down. Raul didn't need to hear them. The truth was she had no feelings for Bastiano.

None.

Yet she did for Raul.

'Not what?' Raul asked.

He's not you would be her honest response.

But rather than say that Lydia was far more evasive. 'He's not what I want.'

'What *do* you want?'

'I wanted what every woman wants, a bit of romance while I was here. I'm not shopping for a husband.' She gave a shrug and pulled one of the tangled sheets from the bed to cover herself. 'I'm going to have a shower.'

And it was in the shower, with space between them, that Lydia pondered what she had been about to say.

He's not you.

With Bastiano there was no attraction. Had it been Raul whom her family were trying to match-make her with she'd have been embarrassed, yes, and annoyed, perhaps, and yet there would have been excitement and trepidation too.

She liked Raul far more than it was safe to let on.

And Raul liked Lydia.

A lot.

That feeling was rare.

Mornings were never his strong point—generally he preferred women who dressed in the dark and were gone. He wasn't proud of that fact, just honest, as he examined his usual wants. Yet this morning he was lying listening to Lydia in the shower and trying to resist joining her.

And again she had surprised him.

Lydia was tough.

There had been no tears, no pleas for help or for him to get involved. In fact she had actively discouraged it when he had offered to step in and deal with Maurice.

There was a level of independence to her that he had seen in few and he did not want her to be gone.

YOUR PARTICIPATION IS REQUESTED!

Dear Reader,

Since you are a lover of our books – we would like to get to know you!

Inside you will find a short Reader's Survey. Sharing your answers with us will help our editorial staff understand who you are and what activities you enjoy.

To thank you for your participation, we would like to send you 2 books and 2 gifts – **ABSOLUTELY FREE!**

Enjoy your gifts with our appreciation,

Pam Powers

**SEE INSIDE
FOR READER'S
SURVEY**

For Your Reading Pleasure...

We'll send you 2 books and 2 gifts
ABSOLUTELY FREE
just for completing our Reader's Survey!

YOUR READER'S SURVEY
"THANK YOU" FREE GIFTS INCLUDE:
▶ **2 FREE books**
▶ **2 lovely surprise gifts**

PLEASE FILL IN THE CIRCLES COMPLETELY TO RESPOND

1) What type of fiction books do you enjoy reading? (Check all that apply)
- ○ Suspense/Thrillers
- ○ Action/Adventure
- ○ Modern-day Romances
- ○ Historical Romance
- ○ Humor
- ○ Paranormal Romance

2) What attracted you most to the last fiction book you purchased on impulse?
- ○ The Title
- ○ The Cover
- ○ The Author
- ○ The Story

3) What is usually the greatest influencer when you <u>plan</u> to buy a book?
- ○ Advertising
- ○ Referral
- ○ Book Review

4) How often do you access the internet?
- ○ Daily ○ Weekly ○ Monthly ○ Rarely or never

5) How many NEW paperback fiction novels have you purchased in the past 3 months?
- ○ 0 - 2
- ○ 3 - 6
- ○ 7 or more

YES! I have completed the Reader's Survey. Please send me the 2 FREE books and 2 FREE gifts (gifts are worth about $10 retail) for which I qualify. I understand that I am under no obligation to purchase any books, as explained on the back of this card.

❏ I prefer the regular-print edition
106/306 HDL GLN5

❏ I prefer the larger-print edition
176/376 HDL GLN5

FIRST NAME	LAST NAME

ADDRESS

APT.#	CITY

STATE/PROV.	ZIP/POSTAL CODE

P-217-SUR17

And, more honestly, he wanted to be her first.

It had nothing to do with Bastiano.

In fact Raul wanted her well away from here.

He was wondering if he could give Lydia what she wanted.

The romantic trip to Italy she craved.

He could do that for a day, surely?

Raul didn't look over at her when Lydia came out from the bathroom and went through to the lounge. There she found her case and pulled out an outfit.

Lydia chose the nice cream dress she had brought for sightseeing and some flat sandals.

Her hair was a bit of a disaster, but she had left her adaptor in her hotel room, so there was no point dragging out her straighteners.

Lydia made do and smoothed it as best she could. She could hear Raul making some calls on his phone and commencing his day.

She had been but a brief interlude, Lydia knew. And so she checked that her sunglasses were in her purse and then walked back into the bedroom—and there he lay. He was even more beautiful now than when she had met him.

Then Raul had been in a suit and clean-shaven.

A mystery.

Now he lay in bed with his hands behind his head, thinking. She knew, because she had lain beside him all night, that he was naked save the sheet that barely covered him. He was unshaven and his eyes seemed heavy from sleep as he turned and looked at her.

And the more that she knew, the more of a mystery he was.

This was regret, Lydia thought.

That he could so easily let her go.

And how did she walk away? Lydia wondered.

How did she go over and kiss that sulky mouth and say goodbye when really she wanted to climb back into bed?

How did she accept that she would never know how it felt to be made love to by him?

But rather than reveal her thoughts she flicked that internal default switch which had been permanently set to 'polite'.

'Thank you so much for last night.'

'I haven't finished being your tour guide yet.'

He stretched out his arm and held out his hand, but Lydia didn't go over. She did not want to let in hope, so she just stood there as Raul spoke.

'It would be remiss of me to let you go home without seeing Venice as it should be seen.'

'Venice?'

Oh, she repeated his offer only because she was mystified. She'd been preparing to leave with her head held high, but then, when she had least expected it, he'd offered more.

So much more.

'I like to call it by its other name—La Serenissima,' Raul said. 'It means the Most Serene.'

'That's not how I remember my time there.'

'Then you have a chance to change that. I'm heading there today. Why don't you come with me? Fly out of Marco Polo tomorrow instead.'

There was another night between now and then, and Lydia knew that even while he offered her an extension he made it clear there was a cut-off.

Time added on for good behaviour.

And Raul's version of 'good behaviour' was that there would be no tears or drama as she walked away. Lydia knew that. If she were to accept his offer, then she had to remember that.

'I'd like that.' The calm of her voice belied the trembling she felt inside. 'It sounds wonderful.'

'Only if you're sure,' Raul added.

'Of course.'

But how could she be sure of anything now she had set foot in Raul's world?

He made her dizzy.

Disorientated.

Not just her head, but every cell in her body seemed to be spinning as he hauled himself from the bed and unlike Lydia, with her sheet-covered dash to the bathroom, his body was hers to view.

And that blasted default switch was stuck, because Lydia did the right thing and averted her eyes.

Yet he didn't walk past. Instead Raul walked right over to her and stood in front of her.

She could feel the heat—not just from his naked body but her own—and it felt as if her dress might disintegrate.

He put his fingers on her chin, tilted her head so that she met his eyes, and it killed that he did not kiss her, nor drag her back to his bed. Instead he checked again. 'Are you sure?'

'Of course,' Lydia said, and tried to make light of it. 'I never say no to a free trip.'

It was a joke—a teeny reference to the very reason she was here in Rome—but it put her in an unflattering light. She was about to correct herself, to say that it hadn't come out as she had meant, but then she saw his slight smile and it spelt approval.

A gold-digger he could handle, Lydia realised.

Her emerging feelings for him—perhaps not.

At every turn her world changed, and she fought for a semblance of control. Fought to convince not just Raul but herself that she could handle this.

They were driven right up to his jet, and his pilot and crew were waiting on the runway to greet them.

'Do you always have a jet on standby?' Lydia asked.

'Always.'

'What's wrong with first class?' Lydia asked, refusing to appear too impressed.

'When children are banned from first class, then I'll consider commercial flights.'

He wouldn't!

Raul liked his privacy, as well as his own staff.

Inside the plane was just as luxurious as the hotel they had come from, and very soon there was take-off and she looked out of the window and watched Rome disappear beneath them.

Lydia felt free.

Excited, nervous, but finally free.

'I travel a lot.' Raul explained the real reason for his plane. 'And, as you saw this morning, my schedule is prone to change. Having my own jet shaves hours off my working week.'

'How did you do all this?' Lydia asked.

'I received an inheritance when my mother died.'

'Your family was rich?'

'No.'

He thought back to Casta. They had been comfortable financially, compared to some, but it had been dirty money and always quickly spent.

Neither the Di Savo nor the Conti wineries had ever really taken off.

And then he thought of him and Bastiano, drinking the wine together and laughing at how disgusting it tasted.

They had been such good friends.

In the anger and hate that had fuelled him for years, Raul had forgotten that part.

It would serve him better not to remember it now.

Bastiano was the enemy, and he reminded himself of that when he spoke next.

'My mother had some money from her brother. She left half to her lover and half to me. It was enough for me to buy the flat I was renting. Then I took out a mortgage on one across the floor and rented it out. I kept going like that. You were right—developers did come in, and they made me an offer that I should not have been able to refuse.'

'But you did?'

'Yes. If they could see the potential, then so could I. One of the owners upstairs had done some refurbishing, and I watched and learnt. By then I had four studio apartments, and I turned them into two more luxurious ones... It had always been an amazing location, but now it was a desirable address. A few years later the other owner and I got the backing to turn it into a hotel. I bought him out in the end. I wanted it for myself. That was always the end game.'

'You used him?'

'Of course,' Raul said. 'That's what I do.'

He didn't care if that put him in an unflattering light.

Better that she know.

'Do you go back often?' Lydia asked. 'To Sicily?'

Raul shook his head. 'I haven't been back since my mother's funeral.

'Don't you miss it?' Lydia pushed.

'There is nothing there for me to miss.'

'You didn't go back for your father's funeral?' Lydia checked.

'No. He was already dead to me.'

'But even so—'

'Should I pretend to care?' Raul interrupted.

Lydia didn't know how to answer that. In her family appearances were everything, and there was a constant demand to be seen to do the right thing.

Raul lived by rules of his own.

'No,' she answered finally.

Her response was the truth—she could think of nothing worse than Raul pretending to care and her believing in his lies.

Better to know from the start that this was just temporary, for when he removed her from his life she really would be gone for good.

'Do you want to change for dinner?'

'Dinner?' Lydia checked, and then she looked at the sun, too low in the sky. The day was running away from them already.

And soon, Lydia knew, it would be her turn to be the one left behind.

CHAPTER EIGHT

LYDIA HAD BEEN in two different bedrooms belonging to Raul.

One at the hotel.

The other on his plane.

Tonight would make it three.

Raul was wearing black pants and a white shirt—dressed for anything, she guessed.

Lydia opened her case, and there was the red dress she had bought with Raul on her mind.

It was too much, surely?

Yet she would never get the chance again. She thought of where she'd be tomorrow—rowing with her mother and no doubt packing a lifetime of stuff into trunks and preparing to move out of the castle.

A bell buzzed, and Lydia knew she had to move a little more quickly.

Simple, yet elegant, there was nothing that should scream 'warning' in the dress, and yet it hugged her curves, and the slight ruching of the fabric over her stomach seemed to indicate the shiver she felt inside.

On sight he had triggered something.

Those dark eyes seemed to see far beyond the rather brittle façade she wore.

She didn't know how to be sexy, yet around him she was.

More than that—she wanted to be.

She added lipstick and wished she'd worn the neutral shoes.

Except Lydia felt far from neutral about tonight.

It was too much.

Far, far too much.

She would quickly change, Lydia decided.

But then there was a gentle rap on the door and she was informed that it was time to be seated.

'I'll just be a few moments,' Lydia said, and dismissed the steward. But what she did not understand about private jets was the fact that there were not two hundred passengers to get strapped in.

'Now.' The steward smiled. 'We're about to come in to land.'

There was no chance to change and so, shy, reluctant, but trying not to show it, Lydia stepped out.

'Sit down,' Raul said.

He offered no compliment—really, he gave no reaction.

In fact he took out his phone and sent a text.

Oddly, it helped.

She had a moment to sit with her new self, away from his gaze, and Lydia looked out of the window and willed her breathing to calm.

Venice was always beautiful, and yet today it was even more so.

As they flew over on their final descent she rose out of the Adriatic in full midsummer splendour, and Lydia knew she would remember this moment for ever. The last time she had felt as if she were sitting alone, even though she had been surrounded by school friends.

Now, as the wheels hit the runway, Lydia came down to earth as her spirit soared high.

And as they stood to leave he told her.

'You look amazing.'

'Is it too much?'

'Too much?' Raul frowned. 'It's still summer.'

'No, I meant...' She wasn't talking about the amount of skin on show, but she gave up trying to explain what she meant.

But Raul hadn't been lost in translation—he had deliberately played vague.

He had heard Maurice's reprimand yesterday morning and knew colour was not a feature in her life.

Till today.

And so he had played it down.

He had told her to sit, as if blonde beauties in sexy red dresses wearing red high heels regularly walked out of the bedroom of his plane.

Actually, they did.

But they had never had him reaching for his phone and calling in a favour from Silvio, a friend.

Raul had been toying with the idea all afternoon... wondering if it would be too much.

But then he had seen her. Stunning in red. Shy but brave. And if Lydia had let loose for tonight, then so too would he.

'Where are we going?' Lydia asked.

'Just leave all that to me.'

Last time she'd been in Venice there had been strict itineraries and meeting points, but this time around there was no water taxi to board. Instead their luggage was loaded onto a waiting speedboat, and while Raul spoke with the driver Lydia took a seat and drank in the gorgeous view.

Then she became impatient to know more, because the island they were approaching looked familiar.

'Tell me where we're going.'

'To Murano.'

'Oh.' Just for a second her smile faltered. Last time Lydia had been there she had felt so wretched.

'Sometimes it is good to go back.'

'*You* don't, though,' Lydia pointed out, because from everything she knew about Raul he did all he could not to revisit the past.

'No, I don't.'

She should leave it, Lydia knew, and for the moment she did.

There was barely a breeze as their boat sliced through the lagoon. Venice could never disappoint. Raul had been right. It heightened the emotions, and today Lydia's happiness was turning to elation.

In a place of which she had only dark memories suddenly everything was bright, and so she looked over to him and offered a suggestion.

'Maybe you should go back, Raul.'

He did not respond.

They docked in Murano, the Island of Bridges, and Raul took her hand to help Lydia off the boat. The same way as he had last night in Rome, he didn't let her hand go.

And in a sea of shorts and summer tops and dresses Lydia *was* overdressed.

For once she cared not.

They walked past all the showrooms and turned

down a small cobbled street. Away from the tourists there was space to slow down and just revel in the feel of the sun on her shoulders.

'I know someone who has a studio here,' Raul said.

He did not explain that often in the mornings Silvio was at Raul's favourite café, and they would speak a little at times. And neither did he explain that he had taken Silvio up on a long-standing offer—'If you ever want to bring a friend...'

Raul had never envisaged that he might.

Oh, he admired Silvio's work—in fact his work had been one of the features that had drawn Raul to buy his home.

He had never thought he might bring someone, though, and yet she was so thrilled to be here, so lacking in being spoilt...

'Silvio is a master glassmaker,' Raul explained. 'He comes from a long line of them. His work is commissioned years in advance and it's exquisite. There will be no three-legged ponies to tempt you.'

And Lydia had never thought she could smile at that memory, yet she did today.

'In fact there is nothing to buy—there is a waiting list so long that he could never complete it in his lifetime. People say that to see him work is to watch the sun being painted in the sky. All we have to do this evening is enjoy.'

'You've never seen him work?'

'No.'

But that changed today.

It was the great man himself who opened a large wooden door and let them in. The place was rather nondescript, with high ceilings and a stained cement floor, and in the middle was a large furnace.

Silvio wore filthy old jeans and a creased shirt and he was unshaven, yet there was an air of magnificence about him.

'This is Lydia,' Raul introduced her.

'Welcome to Murano.'

'She has been here before,' Raul said. 'Though the last time it was on a school trip.'

The old man smiled. 'And did you bring home a souvenir?'

'A vase.' Lydia nodded. 'It was for my mother.'

'Did she like it?'

Lydia was about to give her usual smile and nod, but then she stood there remembering her mother's air of disdain as she had opened the present.

'She didn't seem to appreciate it,' Lydia admitted.

It had hurt a lot at the time.

All her savings and so much pain had gone into the purchase, and yet Valerie had turned up her nose.

But Silvio was looking out of the windows.

'I had better get started. The light is getting low,' he explained.

'Too low to work?' Lydia asked.

'No, no...' He smiled. 'I do very few pieces in a fading light. They are my best, though. I will get some coffee.'

Silvio headed to a small kitchenette and Lydia wandered, her heels noisy on the concrete floor.

There was nothing to see, really, nor to indicate brilliance—nothing to pull her focus back from the past.

'My mother hated that vase,' Lydia told Raul as she

wandered. 'She ended up giving it to one of the staff as a gift.' God, that had hurt at the time, but rather than bring down the mood Lydia shrugged. 'At least it went to practical use rather than gathering dust.'

The coffee Silvio had made was not for his guests, Lydia quickly found out. He returned and placed a huge mug on the floor beside a large glass of water, and then she and Raul had the privilege of watching him work.

Molten glass was stretched and shaped and, with a combination of the most basic of tools and impossible skill, a human form emerged.

And then another.

It was mesmerising to watch—as if the rather drab surroundings had turned into a cathedral. The sun streamed in from the westerly windows and caught the thick ribbons of glass. And Lydia watched the alchemy as somehow Silvio formed two bodies, and then limbs emerged.

It was like witnessing creation.

Over and over Silvio twisted and drew out tiny slivers of glass—spinning hair, eyes, and shaping a slender waist. It was erotic too, watching as Silvio formed breasts and then shaped the curve of a buttock.

Nothing was held back. The male form was made with nothing left to the imagination, and the heat in her cheeks had little to do with the furnace that Silvio used to fire his tools and keep the statue fluid.

It was sensual, creative and simply art at its best. Faces formed and pliable heads were carefully moved, and the kiss that emerged was open-mouthed and so erotic that Lydia found her own tongue running over her lips as she remembered the blistering kisses she and Raul had shared.

It was like tasting Raul all over again and feeling the weight of his mouth on hers.

Lydia fought not to step closer, because she didn't want to get in the way or distract Silvio, yet every minuscule detail that he drew from the liquid glass deserved attention. She watched the male form place a hand on the female form's buttock and flushed as if Raul had just touched her there.

Raul was trying not to touch her.

It was such an intimate piece, and personal too, for it felt as if the energy that hummed between them had somehow been tapped.

And then Silvio merged the couple, pulling the feminine thigh around the male loin, arching the neck backwards, and Lydia was aware of the sound of her own pulse whooshing in her ears.

The erotic beauty was more subtle now, the anatomical details conjoined for ever and captured in glass. And then Silvio rolled another layer of molten glass over them, covering the conjoined beauty with a silken glass sheet.

Yet they all knew what lay beneath.

'Now my signature...' Silvio said, and Lydia felt as if she had been snapped from a trance.

He seared his name into the base, and smoothed it till it was embedded, and then it was for Raul and Lydia to admire the finished piece.

'I've never seen anything like it,' Lydia admitted as she examined the statue.

How could glass be sexy? Yet this was a kiss, in solid form, and the intimate anatomical work that had seemed wasted when the forms had been merged was now revealed—she could see the density at the base of the woman's spine that spoke of the man deep within her.

'It's an amazing piece,' Raul said, and Lydia couldn't believe that his voice sounded normal when she felt as if she had only just returned from being spirited away.

'There are more...' Silvio said, and he took them through to another area and showed them several other pieces.

As stunning as they all were, for Lydia they didn't quite live up to the lovers' statue. Perhaps it was because she had witnessed it being made, Lydia mused as they stepped back out into the street.

It was disorientating.

Lydia went to head left, but Raul took her hand and they went right and he led her back to the speedboat.

The driver had gone, on Raul's instruction, and it was he who drove them to San Marco.

Raul took great pride in showing her around this most seductive of cities.

They wandered through ghostly back streets and over bridges.

'It's so wonderful to be here,' Lydia said. 'It was all so rushed last time, and it felt as if we were just ticking things off a list.'

'And the obligatory gondola ride?' Raul said, but her response surprised him.

'No.' Lydia shook her head. 'Some of the girls did, but...' She stopped.

'But?'

'Sitting on the bus with the teacher was bad enough.

I think a gondola ride with her would have been worse somehow.'

She tried to keep it light, as Raul had managed to when they had been talking about her lonely school trip in Rome. She didn't quite manage it, though.

Raul, who had been starting to think about their dinner reservation, steered her towards the canal.

'Come on,' he said. 'You cannot do Venice without a gondola ride.'

Till this point Raul had, though.

Raul's usual mode of transport was a speedboat.

But there was nothing like Venice at sunset from a gondola, as both found out together.

The low boat sliced gently through the water and the Grand Canal blushed pink as the sun dipped down. He looked over as she sighed, and saw Lydia smiling softly as she drank it all in.

'You don't take photos?' Raul observed.

'My phone's flat,' Lydia said, but then admitted more. 'I'm not one for taking photos.'

'Why not?'

He was ever-curious about her—something Raul had never really been before.

'Because when it's gone it's gone,' Lydia said. 'Best to move on.'

The gondolier took them through the interior canals that were so atmospheric that silence was the best option.

It was cool on the water, and there were blankets they could put over their knees, but she accepted Raul's jacket.

The silk was warm from him, and as she put it on he helped her. The only reason he had not kissed her before was because he'd thought it might prove impossible to stop.

But Raul was beyond common sense thinking now—and so was she.

He took her face in his hands and he looked at her mouth—the lipstick was long gone.

'I want you,' he told her.

'And you know I want you.'

Lydia did.

His mouth told her just how much he wanted her. She watched his eyelids shutter, and then he tasted her. Lydia did the same. She felt the soft weight of him and her mouth opened just a little as they flirted with their tongues. There was tenderness, promise and building passion in every stroke and beat. Yet even as they kissed she cared for the view, and now and then opened her eyes just for a glimpse, because it was like spinning circles in a blazing sky.

His hand slipped inside the jacket. First just the pad of his thumb caressed her breast, and then—she had been right—the dress drew his attention down.

His hand was on her stomach, just lingering, and Lydia felt his warm palm through the fabric. Her breathing stilled and he felt the change and pulled her closer, to taste and feel more.

They sailed under ancient bridges and he kissed her knowingly. So attuned were they no one would guess they weren't lovers yet.

There was just the sound of the gondolier's paddle and the taste of passion.

She was on fire, and yet he made her shiver.

Soon Raul knew the gondolier would turn them around, for the canal ended soon. They were about to pass under the Bridge of Sighs and the bells of St Mark's Campanile were tolling.

Which meant, according to legend, that if they kissed they would be granted eternal love and bliss.

Which Raul did not want.

But their mouths made a fever—a fever neither wanted to break—and anyway he didn't believe in legends.

They pulled their mouths apart as the gondolier turned them around, but their foreheads were still touching.

Lydia was breathless and flushed, and though Raul had made so many plans for her perfect Venetian night he could wait no more.

They should be stopping soon for champagne, and then a canalside dinner at his favourite restaurant. Except his hand was back between them, stroking her nipple through velvet, and her tongue was more knowing.

His best-laid plans were fading.

Lydia pulled her mouth back, but he kissed her cheek and moved his lips towards her ear, and his jaw was rough and delicious, and his hand on her breast had her suddenly desperate.

'Raul…' Lydia said.

Oh, she said his name so easily now.

And he knew her so much more, because there was a slight plea in her voice and it matched the way he felt.

He pulled back his own mouth, only enough to deliver the gondolier an instruction.

The sky was darker as they kissed through the night, and soon they were gliding back towards the

Grand Canal, and now Raul wished for an engine and the speed of his own boat.

The gondolier came to a stop at a water door and said something. It took a moment for Lydia to register that they had stopped and so had the kiss. Realising that she was being spoken to, she looked around breathlessly, staring up at yet another *palazzo* and trying to take in her surroundings.

'It's beautiful!' Lydia said, trying to be a good tourist while wishing they could get back to kissing.

Raul smiled at her attempt to be polite when she was throbbing between the legs.

'It's even more beautiful inside,' Raul told her. 'This is my home.'

Lydia almost wept in relief.

He got out first and took her by the hand, and then pushed open the dark door.

She entered his home an innocent.

Lydia would not be leaving it the same.

CHAPTER NINE

THROUGH THE ENTRANCE and into an internal elevator they went, but Lydia prayed there would be no fire in the night, for she did not take in her surroundings at all—their kisses were frantic and urgent now.

His body was hard against hers, and his hands were a little rough as Raul fought with himself not to hitch up her dress.

The jolt of the old elevator was barely noted—there was just relief that they could get out.

They almost ran.

Raul took her hand and led her with haste through a long corridor lined with ancient mirrors and lit with white pillar candles.

And at the end, as if she were looking through a keyhole, there was the reward of open wooden doors that revealed a vast bed.

She would wake up soon, Lydia was sure.

She would wake up from this sensual dream.

Yet she did not.

There were colours that rained on the walls and the bed, yet she was too into Raul to look for their source.

And was she scared?

No.

Shy?

Not a bit.

Raul stripped, and then no words were needed, no instruction required, as naked, erect, he dealt with her dress.

Lydia held up her hair as he unzipped her.

She shook as he removed the dress, then her bra.

And she moaned as he knelt to remove first her shoes and then the final garment between them.

Raul slid the silk down and probed her with his tongue. Lydia stood and knotted her fingers in his hair, and as Raul gently eased in two fingers, though it hurt, it was bliss.

She parted her legs as he licked and stretched her, and ensured she was oiled at the same time.

He turned away from her then, reaching for the bedside table.

'You're on the Pill?'

Lydia nodded, a touch frantic. She wanted no pause for she needed him inside her.

Lydia had the rest of her life to be sensible and behave.

Just this night.

He took her to his bed and they knelt upon it, kissing and caressing each other. Gliding their hands over each other's body. His muscled and taut…hers softer. They recreated the scene from earlier, at the glassblower's, because it had felt at the time as if they were watching themselves.

'Since we met…' Raul said, and kissed her arched neck.

And her breasts ached for him, but not as much as between her legs.

His erection was pressed against her stomach, nudging, promising, and he wanted to take her kneeling but was aware that it was her first time, and he had felt how tight she was with his fingers.

Raul tried to kiss her into lying down so that he could take things slowly.

She resisted.

And he was glad that she did.

He raised her higher, hooked her leg around him and held himself. And she rested her arms over his shoulders and then lowered herself.

A little.

It hurt, but it was the best hurt.

Raul's eyes were open, and they were both barely breathing, just focused on the bliss they felt.

'Since we met...' he said again, and his voice was low, rich and smoky.

And she lowered herself a little more, and he felt her, tight and hot.

She wanted him so badly but could not see that last bit through. 'Raul...'

There was a plea in her voice again, and he heeded it and took control and thrust hard.

Lydia sobbed as he seared into her. Everything went black, and not just because she'd screwed her eyes closed. She thought she might faint, but he took her hips and held her still and waited as best he could for her to open her eyes.

They opened, and she thought she would never get used to it—ever—but then her breathing evened. And when she opened her eyes again, as she had on the canal, this time they met his.

Raul's hand went to the very base of her spine. His

touch was sensual and she moved a little, slowly, acclimatising to the feel of him within her.

She was sweaty and hot as his hands moved to her buttocks and he started to thrust.

'Raul…'

She wanted him to slow down, yet he *was* moving slowly.

And then Lydia wanted him never to stop.

Pain had left and in its place was a craving, an intense desire for more of what built within.

His hands had guided her into rhythm, but now she found her own. And it was slower than they could account for, for their bodies were frantic, but they relished the intense pleasure. Raul felt the oiled and yet tight grip of her, and each thrust brought him deeper into the mire, to savour or release. Lydia was lost to sensation. His breath in her ear was like music as it combined with the energies concentrated within her.

Her calf ached, but she did not have the will to move it, and then her inner thighs tensed as she parted around him.

The centre of her felt pulled so tight it was almost a spasm, and then she was lost for control and he held her still. And then, when she had thought he could fill her no more, Raul swelled and thrust—rapid and fast.

Lydia screamed, just a little, but it was a sound she had never made before and it came from a place she had never been.

Her legs coiled tight around him, her body hot and pulsing as he filled her.

'Since we met,' he said as she rested her head on his shoulder and felt the last flickers of their union fade, 'I've wanted you.'

'And I you,' Lydia said, for it was the truth.

And then he kissed her down from what felt like the ceiling.

'Res...' Raul said, and then halted and changed what he had been about to say. 'Rest.'

And she lay there in his arms, silent.

Lydia knew there could be no going back from what had just taken place.

And it had nothing to do with innocence lost.

How the hell did she go back to her life without him?

CHAPTER TEN

A GORGEOUS CHANDELIER, creating prisms of light in every shade of spring, was the first thing Lydia saw when she awoke.

There was a long peal of bells ringing out in the distance, but it was a closer, more occasional, deep, sonorous chime that held her attention. It rang low, soft and yet clear, till the sound slowly faded. When it struck again she remembered gliding underneath the Bridge of Sighs with his kiss.

Lydia knew the legend.

She had stood by the bridge with one of her school friends and struck it from her study sheet.

Eternal love and bliss had not applied to her then and it could not now, Lydia knew.

And so she stared up instead and remembered her vow to not show the hurt when it ended.

Pinks, lemons and minty greens dotted the ceiling, and she saw that the beads were actually flowers that threw little prisms of light across the room.

He was awake.

Stretching languorously beside her.

Lydia relished the moment.

His hand slid to her hips and pulled her closer, and

rather than ponder over the fact that soon she would be gone, Lydia chose to keep things light.

'I never pictured you as a man who might have a chandelier in the bedroom.'

Raul gave a low laugh.

He was a mystery, but not hers to solve, and so she did her best to maintain a stiff upper lip.

'A floral chandelier at that,' Lydia added. Her eyes could not stop following the beams of light. 'Though I have to say it's amazing.'

'It drives me crazy,' Raul admitted. 'When I first moved in I considered having it taken down, or changing the master bedroom, but the view of the canal is the best from here.'

'Oh, you can't have it taken down,' Lydia said.

'Easy for you to say. I feel like I am having laser surgery on my eyes some mornings.'

Lydia smiled and carried on watching the light show.

She never wanted to move.

Or rather she did, but only to the beat of their love-making.

His hand was making circles on her stomach and he was hard against her thigh.

Lydia didn't want to check the time just to find out how little time they had left.

'I love your home.'

'You haven't really seen it.'

And she was about to throw him a line about how she could live in just his bedroom for ever, but it would come out wrong, she knew.

He watched the lips he had been about to kiss press together.

Raul saw that.

Then he thought of what he'd been about to say last night.

Restare.

Stay.

He should be congratulating himself for not making such a foolish mistake by uttering that word last night.

Yet the feeling was still there.

And so Raul, far safer than making love to her, as he wanted to, told her how he had come by his home.

'There is a café nearby that I go to. I sometimes see Silvio there, and we chat. On one occasion he told me that this *palazzo* had come on the market. He was not interested in purchasing it but had been to view it as some of his early work was inside.'

I don't care, Lydia wanted to say. *I want to be kissed.*

Yet she did care.

And she did want to know about his home and how he had come by it.

She wanted more information to add to the file marked 'Raul Di Savo' that her heart would soon have to close.

And his voice was as deep as that occasional bell and it resonated in every cell of her body.

She wanted to turn her mouth to feel his, but she lay listening instead.

'Half a century ago it underwent major refurbishment. Silvio made all the internal door handles with his grandfather. But it was the chandelier in the master bedroom that he really wanted to see.'

And now they both lay bathed in the dancing sunbeams of the chandelier as he told its tale.

'It was created by three generations of Silvio's family, long before he was born. I knew that I had to see it, so I called Allegra to arrange a viewing, and then, when I saw it, I had to own it.'

'I can see why.' Lydia sighed. 'I'm back in love with Venice.'

And then she said it.

'I never want to leave.'

It was just what people said at the end of a good trip, Raul knew, but silence hung in the air now, the bells were quiet, and it felt as if even the sky awaited his response.

He needed to think—away from Lydia. For the temptation was still there to say it, to roll into her and make love to her and ask her to remain.

It was unfamiliar and confusing enough for Raul to deal with, let alone her. And so he tried to dismiss the thought in his head that refused to leave.

And Raul knew that Lydia needed her heart that was starting to soar to be reined in.

'People love their holidays,' Raul said. 'I know that. I study it a lot in my line of work. But there is one thing I have consistently found—no matter how luxurious the surroundings, or how fine the cognac, no matter how much my staff do everything they can to ensure the very best stay...' he could see tears sparkle in her eyes and he had never once seen her even close to crying before '...at the end of even the most perfect stay most are ready to go back to their lives.'

'Not always.' Lydia fought him just a little.

And they *both* fought to keep the conversation

from getting too heavy, but they were not discussing holidays—they both knew that.

'I know,' Lydia persisted, 'that when I've had a really good holiday I want more of it…even just a few more days…' She lied, and they both knew it, because Lydia had never had a really good holiday, but he kept to the theme.

'Then that means it was an exceptional trip—a once-in-a-lifetime experience. A guest should always leave wanting more.'

He saw her lips turn white at this relegation and tempered it just a little as he told her they could never be. 'I'll tell you something else I have found—if people do return to that treasured memory it is never quite the same.'

'No.' Lydia shook her head.

'True,' Raul insisted. 'We have couples come back for their anniversary and they complain that the hotel has changed, or that the waterways are too busy, or that the restaurant they once loved is no longer any good… And I know they are wrong, that my hotel has got better since they were there and that the restaurant retains its standard. I know that the waterways of Venice are ever beautiful. It is the couple who have changed.'

'How arrogant of you to assume your guests have no cause for complaint.'

'They don't.'

And as she fought for her belief that all things might be possible, that their slice of time might lead to more, his words thwarted her.

'Why risk spoiling something wonderful?' Raul asked, but when Lydia didn't answer he lay there asking himself the same thing.

Why would he even risk suggesting that she stay?

But didn't guests extend their stays all the time?

Only Lydia wasn't a guest.

He climbed from the bed and attempted to get life back to normal.

'I'm going out for a little while,' Raul told her. 'I'll bring back breakfast.'

Only 'normal' seemed to have left—for Raul never brought back breakfast, and he certainly didn't eat it in bed.

But he had made plans yesterday when she had walked out in that dress. He had sworn to give her the best of Venice, and now it was time to execute that plan.

Then things could get back to normal—once she had gone his head would surely clear.

Lydia, he decided, *wasn't* a guest—she was in fact a squatter who had taken over his long-abandoned heart.

'You'd better call soon to transfer your flight.'

'I will,' Lydia said, glad that he was going out for breakfast. She just needed the space, for the air between them had changed. And she was cross with Raul that he should be able to see her off on a plane after the time they had shared.

And he was cross that he was considering otherwise—that he was *still* considering asking her to stay.

Raul shot her an angry glance as she watched him dress, but she didn't see it. Lydia was too busy watching as he pulled on black jeans over his nakedness.

He looked seedy and unshaven, and he was on the edge of hardening again, and she fought not to pull up her knees as lust punched low in her stomach.

He pulled on black boots, although it was summer,

and then turned to reach for his top. She saw the nail marks on his scarred back and the injury toll from yesterday started to surface.

She was starting to feel sore.

Deliciously so.

'Go back to sleep,' Raul suggested.

He went to walk out, but his resident squatter did what she always did and niggled at his conscience. And so, rather than stalk out, he went over and bent down and gave her a kiss.

They were arguing, Lydia knew.

And she *liked* it.

His jaw scratched as he fought with himself to remove his mouth and get out, and then her tongue was the one to part his lips.

And that perfunctory kiss was no more.

Hellcat.

She made him *want*.

He was dressed and kneeling on the bed, kissing her hard, and she was arching into him.

His hand was rough through the sheet, squeezing her breast hard, and she wanted him to whip the sheet off.

Her hand told the back of his head that.

Lydia wanted him to unzip himself and to feel rough denim.

And so he stopped kissing her and stood.

Raul liked her endless wanting.

And he liked it that he wanted to go back to bed.

And *that* was very concerning to him.

Yes, he needed to think.

'Why don't you go back to sleep?' Raul suggested

again, his voice even and calm, with nothing to indicate the passion he was walking away from.

Apart from the bulge in his jeans.

She gave a slightly derisive laugh at the suggestion that she might find it possible to sleep as he walked to the door.

Raul took the elevator down and, as he always did on a Sunday, drove the speedboat himself. He took it slowly. The sky was a riot of pink and orange, and there was the delicious scent of impending rain hanging heavily in the air.

Her gift would be arriving soon, and Raul badly needed some time alone to think.

Restare.

Stay.

He had almost said it out loud last night but had held back, worried that he might regret it in the light of day. Yet the light was here and the word was still there, on the tip of his tongue and at the front of his thoughts.

Usually he would take breakfast at his favourite café and sit watching the world go by, or on occasion chat with a local such as Silvio.

Not this morning.

He wanted to be home.

On a personal level Raul had never really understood the pleasure of breakfast in bed. He always rose early and, whether home or away, was dressed for the first coffee of the day and checking emails before it had even been poured.

On a business level Raul had both examined and profited from it. There was a lovers' breakfast served at his hotel here in Venice, and a favourite on the menu

was the *baci in gondola*—sweet white pastry melded
with dark chocolate.

Raul was at his favourite café and ordering them
now—only this time he was asking them to be placed
in one of their trademark boxes and tied with a red
velvet ribbon.

It was to be a true lovers' breakfast, because he did
not want maids intruding, and he wanted his coffee
stronger and sweeter than usual today.

Raul wore the barista's eye-roll when he also asked
for English Breakfast Tea.

'Cinque minute, Raul,' the waitress told him.

Five minutes turned into seven, and he was grateful for the extra two, but even when they had passed
still the thought remained.

Restare.

He wanted a chance for them.

Lydia lay, half listening to the sounds of Venice on
a Sunday morning, and thought of their lovemaking.

It was still too close to be called a memory.

Yet it would be soon.

Unless she changed her flight times.

What if she told him she couldn't get a flight out
of Venice until tomorrow?

Lydia got out of bed and pulled on a robe and
found her phone. Even as she plugged it in to charge
it Lydia knew she was breaking the deal they had
made—simply to walk away.

Only it wasn't that simple.

This felt like love.

It was infatuation, Lydia scolded herself.

He was the first person who had shown an interest…

Only that wasn't so.

There had been others, but she had chosen to let no one in.

'Signorina...'

There was a knock at the door and Lydia opened it and smiled at the friendly face of a maid, who said her name was Loretta.

'You have a delivery.'

'Me?' Lydia checked. 'But no one knows that...' And then her voice trailed off, because the name on the box was indeed hers, and as she took it Lydia felt its weight.

There were stickers saying 'Fragile' all over the box and Lydia was trying to reel herself in.

The word was the same in both Italian and English, and she wanted to peel the stickers off and place them on herself.

She was too fragile for this much hope.

Lydia took the box out to the balcony to open it.

It didn't matter that it had started to rain. She needed air, she truly did, because as she peeled back layers of tape and padding, the hopes she had been trying not to get up soared, for there, nestled in velvet, was the art they had seen made.

It was exquisite.

Dark gold it was shot through with colour, red and crimson, and she ran her fingers along the cool glass and recalled the way Raul had held her last night.

It was more than a gift, and far more than the once-promised morning-after present, surely—it felt like a diary of *them*.

The kisses and caresses...the oblivion they had

found…the melding of two bodies. It was the most beautiful thing she had ever seen, let alone been given.

How could she even hope to hold on to her heart? Lydia thought, and then she looked out on the canal and there he was, steering the boat with ease, the man she loved.

Loved.

Her own admission scared her.

Raul didn't want her love.

She felt that if he so much as looked up he might read her, so Lydia gathered the box and the statue and went back into the room and attempted to reel herself in.

It was a gift.

An exceptionally generous gift.

It didn't necessarily mean that he felt the same and she had to remember that.

She was trying to hold on to that thought so hard that when her phone rang, unthinkingly Lydia took the call.

'You fool.'

That was how Maurice greeted her, and Lydia pulled the phone back from her ear, about to turn it off, because she refused to let him ruin this day.

But, having called her a fool, Maurice then asked her a question.

'What the hell are you doing with Raul Di Savo?' Maurice asked.

'That's not your concern.'

He'd never told her his surname, though she had seen it on the business card he had given her.

More concerning was how Maurice had known.

But, unasked, he told her. 'There are pictures of the two of you all over the Net.'

'Us?'

'Have you *any* idea of the fire you're playing with? He's using you, Lydia.'

That much she knew wasn't true.

Lydia looked at the statue he had bought her, the most beautiful gift ever given, and she recalled not just Raul's touch but how even without words he made her feel good about herself.

Even if their time was to be fleeting, for once in her life someone had truly liked her.

That was the real gift.

'He isn't *using* me,' Lydia sneered, utterly confident in that statement.

She had gone willingly, after all.

And then everything changed.

'He just wants to get at Bastiano.'

She was so sick of hearing that man's name. 'What the hell does Bastiano—' And she stopped, for in that second Lydia answered her own question.

Even before Maurice told her outright, Lydia already knew.

'They were friends until Bastiano had an affair with his mother. Raul has sworn to make him pay slowly… Screwing you was mere revenge.'

Hope died silently, Lydia found out as she stood there.

No protest.

No flailing.

For Maurice's filthy term matched her thoughts.

She *had* been screwed.

It made sense.

Well, better sense than that she might ever be loved for herself.

She ended the call and looked for the photos Maurice had alluded to. Her heart was thumping…she knew that soon Raul would be back.

There was only one photo she could find—they were in that Rome café, drenched in the morning sun, and he was holding her hand.

She had been innocent then.

And Lydia wasn't thinking about sex.

She had been innocent of the level of hurt he might cause, for she had sworn she would let no one close ever again.

Oh, she was a fool—for she had.

So, *so* close.

Lydia wanted to retch as she thought of their lovemaking, and she held in a sob as she had a sudden vision of herself coming undone under his expert ministrations.

Had he been laughing on the inside?

Everything was tainted black.

Her phone rang again, and Lydia saw that it was Arabella.

She must have seen the photos.

Lydia was no doubt popular now.

'Hey…' Arabella said. 'When are we going to catch up? How about tonight?'

'I can't make it.'

'Well, soon?'

'No, thank you.'

'When, then?'

'I've got to go.'

Lydia gave no reason.

Raul had taught her that much at least.

She ended the call and ran to the balcony and stood there dragging in air and trying to fathom how to face the man who had destroyed her.

Would he be like Arabella and barely flinch when he found he'd been caught out?

All her confidence was shredded.

She was no butterfly emerging, Lydia knew, but a dragonfly.

Didn't they spread their wings for just one day?

Her wings were gone now, torn and stripped, and it hurt to be bare.

She stood clutching the stone balcony in the rain and wondered if she had time to pack and get out. But it was too late. She looked down and saw the empty speedboat and knew he must be on his way up.

Leaving without tears, leaving with pride, wasn't just a wish but an imperative now—Raul must *never* know the hurt he had caused her, Lydia vowed.

Not one tear would she give him.

She would have been better off with Bastiano!

At least there she had known the score.

A whore, albeit with a ring on her finger.

And then it came to her—Lydia knew how to hurt Raul now.

CHAPTER ELEVEN

'HEY...'

She turned and saw him. His hair was wet, and had she not found out, Lydia knew they would have been naked soon.

Why did he have to be so beautiful?

How she wished there had been just another day till she'd found out.

'Why are you standing in the rain?' Raul asked.

'I was just taking in the view before I go.'

'About that...'

'I called and they can transfer my flight, but I have to leave soon.'

'You don't.' Raul shook his head. He had a jet on call, after all, but more than that he wanted to say it.

Stay.

'Come and have breakfast and we can talk.'

'No, thanks,' Lydia said, and she wondered herself how she did it, because she actually managed to smile.

She had at her father's funeral as she had thanked the guests for coming.

And she had smiled at Arabella that awful day in Murano as she had purchased the vase.

No one knew her, and now she would make sure no one ever did.

Yes, her innocence was gone.

In every sense.

'I have a lot to sort out, Raul. I need to get home and face things.'

'I know that, but it can wait a few days. Come inside—I brought breakfast.'

And Lydia knew she wasn't that good an actress. She could not lie in bed and eat. And so she shook her head. 'I need to go, Raul.'

He kissed her to change her mind.

And she let him.

Desperate for the taste of him just one more time.

He nudged with his hips, he cajoled with his tongue, and he nearly won.

'Come on.'

He led her inside, but instead of going to bed Lydia reached for her case and placed it on the bed and started to pack.

'I don't get why you're leaving,' Raul said. He did not understand her mood.

'Wasn't it you who said I don't need to give an excuse or a reason?'

Indeed it had been.

And so he watched as she put the red shoes into the case, and the underwear he had peeled off last night, and selected fresh for today.

Her robe was clinging and her nipples were thick, and Lydia, as she went and unplugged her phone, did not understand how she could both hate and want.

'Can we talk?' Raul said.

'And say what?' Lydia asked, and there was strain to her voice.

'I don't want you to leave yet.'

A few moments ago she would have knelt at his feet for those words, now she turned angrily.

'Oh, sorry—were you hoping for a morning shag because you bought me a statue?'

Oh, it wasn't her wings growing back—it was nails. Thick steel nails that shot out like armour.

'Raul, thank you so much for your hospitality. I had a wonderful time.'

'That's it?'

And she did know how to hurt him!

'I think we both know I was never going to be leaving Italy a virgin. It was you or Bastiano. I chose you.'

He stood there silent, Raul did not ask why, yet Lydia answered as if he had.

'Bastiano isn't what I want.'

'And what is?'

'Money.'

'He has that.'

She screwed up her nose. 'I want old money.'

'I see.'

'If I'm to marry for money I'd at least like a title.'

'You're a snob.'

'I have every right to be.'

'And a gold-digger,' Raul said.

'Yes!' Lydia smiled a black smile. 'I'm a snob *and* a gold-digger, and some Sicilian who just made good doesn't really do it for me.'

'You make no sense, given the way you screamed last night.'

'We're talking about Bastiano,' Lydia said. 'As you

pointed out—he wanted marriage and a nice trophy wife. I, on the other hand, wanted sex.' She ran a finger along his jaw and taunted him and it felt so good. 'For a one-night stand, you were the far better option. What I *really* want is a gentleman.'

'Well.' He gave a black smile and removed her hand from his face. 'I don't qualify, then.'

'No.'

He dropped all contact, and as she turned and walked away suddenly Lydia wasn't so brave.

As she bent to retrieve her red dress and picked it up from the floor, it felt as if she was waving a flag to a very angry bull, though Raul did not move.

His hackles were up. Raul could fight dirty when he chose—and he was starting to choose to now.

He looked at her slender legs and her hair falling forward and knew she could feel his eyes on her body as she pretended to concentrate on folding the dress as she bent over the open case.

She was pink in the cheeks and her ears were red, and as his eyes took in the curve of her bottom he knew she was as turned on as he was.

Tension crackled between them and she could almost picture his hands pulling up her robe.

It was bizarre.

He made filthy thoughts mandatory, gave anger a new outlet, and she recalled his promise that angry sex could wait.

'You know,' he said, 'once you leave, you're gone. I don't play games, and I don't pursue…'

'I'm not asking you to.'

He walked over—she heard him but did not turn around. She must have folded that dress twenty times when his hand came to her hip. Just a small gesture, almost indicating that she should turn to him, but Lydia resisted.

'Hey, Lydia,' he said, and he bent over her and spoke in that low, calm voice, while hard against her bottom. 'When you find your suitably titled Englishman, don't think of me.'

'I shan't.'

'It would not be fair to him.'

'You really—' She stopped, and she dared not turn around, for now one hand moved to her waist and the other to her shoulder, and there was a desire in Lydia for the sound of his zip, but it never came.

'When you're in bed,' Raul said, and she held on to the bed with cheeks flaming, 'and he says, "Is that nice, darling?" or "Do you like it like that?"' He put on an affected tone. 'Try not to remember that I never needed to enquire. And,' he added cruelly, 'when you lie there beside him, unsated, and you *do* think of me...'

'I told you—I shan't.'

'Liar.'

He pressed into her one more time and then pulled back and let her go and she straightened up.

She was a bit breathless.

Oh, and still angry.

She pulled off her robe and he did not avert his eyes. He watched as she pulled on knickers, and watched as she put on her bra.

And he watched as she pulled on the taupe dress—the one with the buttons.

Bloody things!

As she struggled to dress he walked over—but not

to her. This time he picked up the statue and tossed it into her case.

'I don't want your stupid statue.'

'I thought you were a gold-digger,' he pointed out. 'Sell it.' Raul shrugged. 'Or hurl it out of the window of your turret in frustration when your fingers can't deliver.'

'Oh, *please*,' Lydia sneered. 'You think you're *so* good.'

'No,' Raul said. 'I *know* that we were.'

He did.

For he had never experienced it before—that absolute connection and the erotic bliss they had found last night.

She snapped her case closed and, rather annoyingly, set the security code on the lock.

As she bumped it from the bed he kicked off his boots and got on. Raul lay on the rumpled sheets and reached for his cake box and took out his phone.

She could see herself out, Raul decided.

The private jet was closed.

Lydia stood there for a moment. It was hard making a dignified exit when you didn't know the way out.

'Is there a street entrance?' Lydia asked, and watched as he barely glanced up from his phone.

'Yep.'

Raul opened the box of pastries and selected one, took a bite as he got back to his phone.

Lydia could find it herself.

'You can see yourself out.'

CHAPTER TWELVE

ALL ROADS LED to Rome.

But today Raul hoped that Rome would lead him to Lydia.

Raul could not get her out of his mind.

Disquiet gnawed and unfinished business reared up and he simply could not let it go.

Summer was gone.

As he walked past the café where they had shared breakfast Raul looked up to the dark clouds above and it looked as if the sky had been hung too low.

It had felt like that since Lydia had gone.

Autumn had arrived, and usually it was Raul's favourite time of the year.

Not this one.

He missed her, and Raul had never missed anyone, and he just could not shake off the feeling.

It was something he could not define.

Even if the tourists never really thinned out in Venice, La Serenissima had felt empty rather than serene. Here in Rome the locals were enjoying the slight lull that came with the change. Back in Sicily the vines that threaded the valley would be turning to russet...

Raul never went back.

Not even in his head.

Yet he was starting to now.

Lydia had been right—perhaps he should go back.

If this visit to the Grande Lucia did not work out as he hoped, then Raul would be making his first trip back to Casta since the will had been read.

The doorman nodded as Raul went through the brass revolving door, and he stood for a moment remembering their brief time there.

But that was not right. It didn't *feel* brief—if anything it was the most examined part of his life.

Lydia was the most contrary person he knew.

Cold and guarded…warm and intense.

And, although they had both agreed to a one-night stand, he still could not make sense of that morning.

That kiss before he had left to get breakfast had held promise, but Raul had returned to a stranger and he *had* to know why.

But he didn't even know her surname.

Raul knew some of the darkest most intimate parts of Lydia, and yet her full name he did not know.

Nor where she lived.

Usually those details did not matter to him.

Oh, but they did now.

He had searched, and so had Allegra.

There were a surprising number of castles in England, and there were many that were used for weddings.

They had got nowhere.

Allegra was working her way through them all and had flown over to England three times.

And now Raul was in Rome.

Back at the Grande Lucia, where it had all started.

Now that Raul was showing no interest in purchasing the hotel he was having trouble getting through to Sultan Alim.

And so he was here in person.

But trouble remained in the shape of the young receptionist.

'Sultan Alim is only available by appointment.'

'Call and tell him that Raul Di Savo is here.'

'As I said, he only sees people by appointment. We don't disturb him with phone calls.'

She was as snooty and as immutable as he demanded that Allegra should be if someone—anyone—tried to invade Raul's time.

'Is he even in the country?' Raul asked, but that information was off-limits.

'He would prefer that we do not discuss his movements. I shall let him know you were here.'

Now what?

Did he sit in the foyer and wait for a royal sultan who might already be back in the Middle East? Or warn the poor receptionist that if she valued her job she should let Alim know...

And then Raul saw someone who might be able to help.

She was walking through the foyer carrying a huge display of roses.

Gabi.

The indiscreet wedding planner!

'Hey,' Raul said.

'Hi.'

He had forgotten how to flirt—even for gain.

'Gabi?'

'Oh!' She stopped. 'You were in the ballroom when Alim…' Her voice trailed off.

There had been something going on that afternoon. Raul knew it. He hadn't given it much thought until now.

'I'm hoping to meet with him.'

'Good luck!' Gabi rolled her eyes. 'He's back home.'

'Oh!'

'For his wedding.'

'I see.'

'I'm planning it, actually.'

She looked as if she were about to cry.

'Can you let him know I need to speak with him?'

'I'm a wedding planner,' Gabi said. 'I don't get access to the Royal Sultan.'

And neither would he, Raul thought as Gabi flounced off.

So that left Bastiano—and Raul already knew where *he* was.

Casta.

His jet landed at Cosimo airport, and though it was warmer the sky still seemed to be hung too low. Raul put on his shades and transferred to the helicopter he had arranged to take him to the old convent.

To afford the nuns seclusion it had been made accessible only by horse or helicopter.

Of course Raul chose the latter.

The convent was an ancient sprawling building that no one could get to, set on the crest of the valley overlooking the wild Sicilian Strait.

Its inaccessibility made it the perfect retreat, and Raul had to hand it to Bastiano for his foresight.

Not that he would admit that.

Raul boarded the helicopter and saw his orders had been followed. There was a bunch of lilies there, which, after meeting with Bastiano, he would take to Maria's grave.

He would arrive unannounced.

Raul had sworn never to return.

Only for Lydia he did.

It would be kinder, perhaps, not to look out of the helicopter window and at first he chose not to. The last time he had been home it had been on a commercial flight and then a frantic taxi ride to the valley.

Raul had been eighteen then, and he recalled the taxi driver asking him to pay the fare in advance before agreeing to take him.

Different times.

Same place.

He looked, and the view was starting to become familiar. Even if he had never seen it from this vantage point, the lie of this land was etched on the dark side of his soul.

There were the fields that the Contis and Di Savos had fought over for generations, and yet the wine had never made either family their fortune—and Raul's palate now knew it never would.

His stomach turned in on itself, and it had nothing to do with the sudden banking of the chopper, more the view of the schoolyard, and beyond it to what had been his family home.

He could hear his childish lies to his father.

'Mamma has been here all day.'

Or…

'I think she went to breakfast with Loretta.'

And now perhaps he understood why Lydia did not take photos, for there were memories you did not want to see.

Raul hadn't lied just to save himself.

He had lied to cover for his mother.

Over and over and over.

And then he recalled her more cheerful dispositions. When she would sing and start to go out more, and Raul's lies to his father would have to begin again.

There was the church, and to the side the tombstones.

Raul's history stretched beneath him and there was nothing he wanted to see.

But he made himself look.

The ocean was wild and choppy, crashing onto jagged rocks, and then he saw it.

Far from falling into disrepair the old convent now stood proud, and he remembered his mother's tears when it had closed down.

Had it really been her dream?

The chopper landed and Raul climbed out.

He thought Security might halt him, but he walked across the lush lawn and towards the gateway without confrontation.

There was a sign for Reception and Raul headed towards it. He walked past a fountain and then ignored the bell and pushed open a heavy arched door.

There were downlights—a modern touch that softened the stone walls—and at a desk sat a young woman wearing what looked like a dental nurse's uniform.

'Posso aiutarla?'

With a smile she asked Raul if she could help him.

'Si.' Raul nodded. 'I am here to speak with Bastiano.'

No frown marred her Botoxed brow, but Raul could see the worry in her eyes as she checked the computer, even though her smile stayed in place.

'May I have your name?'

'Raul Di Savo...'

She must be just about due to have her anti-wrinkle injections topped up, for now a line formed between her brow and the smile faded.

Oh, that name—even now—was known in the valley.

'Do you have an appointment?'

'No,' Raul responded. 'He isn't expecting me...'

'On the contrary.'

Bastiano's voice arrived before he did, and Raul looked up as he emerged from the shadows of the archway. A glint of sun captured the scar on his cheek, and Raul thought he looked like the devil himself appearing.

'Bastiano.' Raul didn't even attempt to keep the ice from his voice. 'I would like to speak with you.'

'I rather thought that you might,' Bastiano said, his response equally cool. His indubitable charm would never be wasted on Raul. 'Come this way.'

Raul followed him through the arch and they walked along a cloister that looked down on a quadrangle where a small group were sitting in the afternoon sun, talking. They glanced up at the two dark-suited men, for there was a foreboding energy about them that drew attention.

Even the receptionist had followed, and stood watching as they disappeared into the old refectory.

The darkness was welcome, and the windows were

like photo frames, setting off a view of the Sicilian Strait that roared in the distance.

'Take a seat,' Bastiano offered.

It would be churlish to stand, Raul knew, when he was here for a favour, so as Bastiano moved behind his desk Raul sat at the other side.

'There is something I need from you,' Raul said. 'I would have preferred not to just land on you, but you refused to take my calls.'

Bastiano didn't say anything, but Raul saw the smile of triumph that he attempted to contain. Of course he would not take Raul's calls—he would far prefer to witness him beg.

'I didn't return your calls because I don't think I can help you, Raul,' Bastiano answered, and his manicured hand gestured to some papers on the desk before him. 'Alim said you have been trying to reach him. I know how badly you wanted the hotel, but a deal has been reached—the contracts are awaiting my signature.'

Bastiano thought he was here about the Grande Lucia, Raul realised.

But then why *wouldn't* he think that?

A few weeks ago that had been all that had mattered to Raul—acquisitions, pipping Bastiano to the post and amassing the biggest fortune.

'I'm not here about the hotel,' Raul said, and he watched as Bastiano's contained features briefly showed his confusion.

But he righted himself quickly.

'So what is it that you want?'

'You were considering investing in a property in the UK.' Raul attempted to be vague, but it did not work.

'I have many investments there.'

'It was a castle.'

Raul knew the exact second that Bastiano understood the reason for his visit, for now he made no effort to contain his black smile as he spoke. 'I don't recall.'

'Of course you do.' Raul refused to play games. 'If you could give me the details I would be grateful.'

'I don't require your gratitude, though.'

He had been mad to come, Raul realised.

But then mad was how he *had* been of late.

And now he sat in front of his nemesis, asking him for help.

Worse, though, there were other questions he wanted to ask him. Bastiano held some of the keys to his past.

A past Raul did not want to examine.

Yes, this was madness, Raul decided.

No more.

He stood to leave and did not even bother making the right noises, for there was nothing even to pretend to thank Bastiano for.

But as he reached the door Bastiano's voice halted him.

'There is something I want.'

Raul did not turn around and Bastiano continued.

'If you return the ring I'll give you the information.'

Still Raul did not turn around, though he halted. He actually fought not to lean on the door, for he felt as if the air had been sucked out of the room. He was back in the courtroom, staring at that emerald and seed pearl ring and wondering from where it had come.

Gino had given his mother nothing other than a

thin gold band that might just as well have been a ball and chain, for in Maria's eyes it had held her to him for life…

Not quite.

She had been unfaithful, after all.

Then Bastiano spoke. 'I gave it to your mother the week before she died. It belongs in my family…'

'Why did you give her the ring?' Raul turned.

'She said that she wanted to leave Casta and be with me. The ring secured our plans.'

'You expect me to believe that you two were in *love*?' Raul sneered.

'I thought so for a while.' Bastiano shrugged. 'It was really just sex.'

Raul was across the room in an instant, and he reached out to upend the table just to get to Bastiano, but somehow the bastard had him halting, for he held out a pen as if it were a knife.

'I want my ring,' Bastiano said.

And the pen in his hand was the only thing preventing Raul from slamming him against the stone wall and exacting his final revenge.

'You'll get it.'

Bastiano wrote down the details, but, as he did, he said something that a few years ago would have had Raul reaching again for his throat.

Now it made Raul feel sick.

'Don't make her a saint, Raul,' Bastiano said. 'She was far from that.'

Raul felt as if his head was exploding as he walked out.

The helicopter's rotors started at the pilot's sight of him and Raul ran across the ground.

It took minutes.

Barely minutes,

And he was standing at his mother's grave.

It should feel peaceful—there was just the sound of birds and the buzzing of his phone—but the roar in his ears remained.

It had never left.

Or rather it had dimmed in the brief time he and Lydia had shared.

Now he turned off his phone, and it felt as if even the birds were silent as he faced the truth.

Bastiano had not been the first affair.

He had been the last.

And there had been many.

Raul had been taught to lie—not just to save himself but to cover for his mother.

He looked back to the convent and remembered her tears when it had closed and her misery. Then he recalled her being more cheerful, when her mood would lift for a while. And while it would make most children happy to see their mother smile, Raul had known that if he were to keep her safe, then the lies had to start again.

Maria Di Savo.

Unhinged, some had called her.

'Fragile' was perhaps a more appropriate word.

At least it was the one Raul chose.

But with more open eyes than the last time he had stood here.

'Rest now,' he said to the stone, and he went to lay the lilies.

But then he divided them into two.

And he turned to the grave of Gino Di Savo.

There was someone he had never considered forgiving—it had been so far from his mind as to be deemed irrelevant.

It was more than relevant now.

Was Gino even his father?

Sixteen and pregnant in the valley would have been a shameful place to be.

Had the younger Gino been kinder?

Had he lived with the knowledge of constant infidelity?

Perhaps Raul would never know.

He understood the beatings more, though.

And maybe there were some respects to be paid.

'Rest now,' Raul said again, and he put the remaining lilies on Gino Di Savo's grave.

CHAPTER THIRTEEN

'IT'S A VERY recent piece.'

The valuation manager had called in the director. And Lydia was starting to get a glimpse of just how valuable the statue was.

'Three months,' Lydia said, but they didn't look over at her.

For the first morning in a very long time Lydia had held down some toast and decided it was time to be practical and deal with things.

Lydia had returned to the castle expecting anger and recrimination, and had been ready to get the hell out.

Instead she'd returned to her mother's devastation.

It wasn't only Lydia who hadn't cried on her father's death.

Valerie too had held it in, and finally the dam had broken.

'I'm sorry!' She had just slumped in a chair and cried. 'I've told him he's never to come back.'

Of all the hurts in Lydia's heart, Maurice didn't rank, and so instead of fighting back or getting out Lydia had done what Raul had done. She'd poured her mother a drink and stayed calm.

She'd been her practical self, in fact, and had put her own hurts aside.

Lydia pulled the castle as a wedding venue and then dealt as best as she could with what was.

There was no money and very little left to sell.

Last week she had suggested that Valerie go and spend some time with her sister.

Lydia needed to be alone.

She was pregnant.

But she did have her mother's practical nature and had decided to find out what the statue was worth.

Not to save the castle.

Raul was right—it would require a constant infusion.

The proceeds of the sale of the statue might at least go towards a deposit on a house.

But then the valuation manager had called for the director and numbers had started to be discussed between the men.

Lydia realised she had far more than a deposit.

In fact she could buy a home.

It was worth that much and very possibly more.

She could provide for her baby and Raul didn't even need to know.

'Are you thinking of the New York auction?' the manager was asking his senior.

'That's a few months off.'

He glanced over to Lydia and offered her an option.

'I have several collectors who would be extremely interested—we could run a private auction. This piece is exquisite.'

And she loved it so.

It was just a piece of glass, Lydia told herself.

There was a reason she didn't take photos—going over old memories hurt too much.

She would be better rid of it, Lydia knew, and yet it was the only thing she had ever loved.

Apart from Raul.

He wasn't a thing—he was a person.

An utter bastard, in fact.

But the statue spoke of a different time, before it had all fallen apart, and Lydia could not stand the thought of letting it go.

Over and over she dissected each moment with him.

At every minute her mind was back there, peeping through the keyhole he had once shown her and seeing them.

Every moment was captured, and yet she had no photos, bar the one of them holding hands that was smeared all over the internet.

Apparently the great Raul did not usually stoop to holding hands, so the press had been interested.

She'd been telling him about her father then.

Confiding in him.

And he had been playing her all along.

All she had of him was this statue.

No, Lydia corrected, in six months' time she would have his baby.

And Raul needed to know.

The director finally addressed her. 'With your permission I'm going to make a few phone calls, and then perhaps we'll be able to see more where we're at.'

'Of course,' Lydia agreed.

And so must she make some calls.

Lydia was shown to a comfortable waiting room that was more like a lounge and offered tea.

'No, thank you,' Lydia said as she took a seat. 'Could you please close the door?'

The door was closed and from her purse Lydia took out the business card he had given her.

It had been three months since Lydia had heard his voice.

The business card had had many outings, but always she'd bailed before completing his number.

Today Lydia held her breath as she was finally put through.

He didn't answer.

It was just a recording—telling her to leave a message. *'Lasciate un messagio...'*

An anti-climax, really, and yet the sound of his voice had her folded over in the chair.

Not because of what she had to say to him, but because of what she wanted to.

That even while she was so terribly angry with him, it was the hurt of not seeing him, not hearing him, not touching him that refused to heal.

She didn't know what to do.

How did you tell a man who would have a baby removed from a restaurant for crying that you were pregnant with his child?

Raul would think she was calling for money.

How could he not, given she had looked him in the eye and *told* him she was a gold-digger?

And a snob.

Oh, she had to play the part now. But she couldn't and so rang off.

Straighten up, she told herself, and reminded herself of the terrible things he had done.

Raul had used her so badly.

He had sunk to such depraved lows and she must always remember that.

Always.

Panic was starting to build, but Lydia took a deep breath and told herself to be practical and deal with things.

So she straightened up in the chair and repeated the call.

'Lasciate un messagio...'

'Raul, this is Lydia.'

She refused to cheapen herself by giving him dates and further details. If Raul was such a playboy that he didn't remember her, then she wasn't going to make things easier for him.

'I'm pregnant.'

She had said it too fast and too soon, Lydia knew that, but better that than to break down.

'I've had a few weeks to get used to the idea, and I'm actually...' She let out her first calm breath—maybe because she'd told him now...maybe because she was speaking the truth. 'I'm fine with it. We'll be fine. The baby and I, I mean.'

And she knew that had sounded too brusque.

'What I'm trying to say is that I'm not calling for support, neither on an emotional nor financial front. We both know you don't do the former, and I've had the statue valued and it covers the latter...'

Not quite.

Yes, no doubt she could squeeze him for half of his billions, but it was not the route she wanted to take.

The thought of lawyers and acrimony, of whether or not he believed her, were the last things she wanted.

'If you need to discuss things, then give me a call back.'

Lydia ended the call and sat staring at her phone for a very long time.

His reaction she could not fathom, and, for the first time since arriving back in England, Lydia felt grateful for the distance between them.

He knew now.

CHAPTER FOURTEEN

SHE WAS IN a holding pattern now of her own making.

Awaiting his response.

Once home, Lydia had replaced the statue by her bed.

She had decided that it was not for sale.

Some things *were* more important.

For now.

She did not want to be like her mother, holding on to a castle she could not afford to keep, but she was not going to rush into selling it.

Lydia checked her phone for the hundredth time, but of course it hadn't rung.

So she checked her email to see if anyone had responded to her many job applications.

She'd had one interview at a museum, but there were four other applicants—no doubt all with qualifications.

And she had an interview next week to work at one of their rival wedding venues.

Joy.

Not.

The pregnancy would start to show soon.

Who would want to take her on then?

Lydia opened a window and leant out and looked over the land her mother's family had owned for ever.

The hills to the left and the fields to the right had been sold off some time ago, but if she looked ahead it was still theirs—for now.

And she understood her mother a little better, for she knew it hurt so much to let go.

Lydia heard the low buzz of a helicopter and looked to the sky.

It was a familiar sound in these parts—the well-heeled left for London in the morning and returned in the evening, but usually later than now.

Occasionally there was an air ambulance or a tourist.

Except this helicopter hovered over the castle and the buzzing sound grew louder.

She could see the grass in the meadow moving in the swirl the rotors created.

It was Raul who was descending, Lydia knew.

Not for *her*.

He'd had weeks and months to find *her*.

No, she had dropped the baby bombshell and he had responded immediately.

He was here about their child.

Her breath quickened as he climbed out. He was wearing a dark suit and tie and shades. He looked completely together as he strode across the land with purpose and she watched him.

There was no instinct to hide.

If anything her instinct was to descend the stairs and run towards him, but that would show just how much she had missed him.

Raul didn't need to know that.

And neither would she tell him that she knew about his long-running feud with Bastiano.

Yes, Lydia was far from innocent now.

Knowledge was power, and she would use it wisely.

And she would never reveal how deeply she had loved.

So she did not check her reflection, nor bother to don lip gloss. Instead she descended the circular stairs of the turret and walked through to the main entrance.

Neither did she go through the palaver of making him knock.

The door was heavy, but she opened it with practised ease. The days of having staff to attend to such things were long since gone.

'Raul…' She hesitated, because unlike her earlier summation she saw he *wasn't* quite so together. There was a grey pallor to his face and his jaw was tense. His eyes remained hidden behind dark shades. 'I wasn't expecting you.'

'Then you don't know me.'

Those words sent a shiver of warning down her spine.

No, she didn't know him—but those words told her the news she had so recently broken to him was being taken very seriously indeed.

'Were you already in England?'

'No.'

Raul had been walking away from the cemetery when he had heard her message.

'Oh…' The speed of his arrival was rapid, but then she had only been privy to his casual use of his private jet but once.

'I'm sorry for the shock.'

'Nobody has died, Lydia.'

Raul was right. It was a pregnancy they were dealing with, after all, not a sudden death, and yet it was surely a shock to a man like him—a confirmed bachelor, a reprobate playboy.

Or maybe not, Lydia mused.

Perhaps he had illegitimate children dotted all over the world, for certainly he seemed to be taking rapid control.

'We need to talk.'

'Of course we do,' Lydia said. 'That's why I called. Come through and I'll make some tea.'

She would take him to the receiving room, Lydia decided. It was a little faded and empty, but it was certainly the smartest room. There she would ask him to take a seat, and then go and make some tea, and then they could calmly discuss...

Fool.

'I don't drink tea, Lydia.'

As she went to walk away his hand closed around the top of her arm, and Lydia actually kicked herself for thinking she could so easily dictate this.

'Coffee, then?'

She received a black smile in response.

'The helicopter is waiting to take us to my jet—we shall discuss this in Venice.'

'Venice?' She shook her head, her attempt to deal with him calmly, disintegrating. 'Absolutely not. We can talk here. My mother is at her sister's and Maurice is gone.'

His features did not soften.

'We can go out for tea if you prefer. If that makes you feel...'

She did not get to finish.

'You think we are going to sit in some quaint café and discuss the future of our child?'

'We could!'

'And what time does this café close?' He watched her jaw clench and then continued. 'We have a lot to sort out, dear Lydia.' The term was without endearment. 'Did you really think you could drop a message like that on my phone and expect us to go out for *afternoon tea*?'

'I thought we could calmly discuss—'

'I am calm.'

He didn't sound it to Lydia.

Oh, his words were calm, but there was an undercurrent, an energy that danced in the grand entrance hall and not even these ancient walls could contain it.

'We shall speak at my home.'

'No!'

'Okay, we'll talk at my office.'

'In Venice?'

'Of course.'

'No.'

'Lydia, what time to you have to be at work tomorrow?' Raul asked, guessing she probably hadn't bothered to get a job.

'That wasn't kind.'

'I'm not here to be kind.'

She glimpsed again his power and knew this man did not fight fair.

He proved it now.

'I thought you said you were leaving home and getting a job…' He gave a black laugh as he looked around. 'But you're still here, and of course you don't need to work now.'

'Raul…' She wanted to take back that gold-digger comment, but it was way, way too late. 'Please listen—it was an accident.'

'Of course it was!'

She could almost taste his sarcasm.

'Lydia, unlike you, I *do* have to work—however, I have set aside an hour tomorrow at eleven for us to start to go through things. If you don't want to fly with me, fine, but can you get yourself there, at least?'

'I'm not going to be there, Raul.'

'Then we do this through lawyers. Text me the name of yours.'

He was done.

Raul was not going to stand there and plead.

His head was throbbing.

The events of today—Bastiano, the revelations about his mother, his father, if Gino had even been his father, and now the fact that he himself was going to be a father…

Hell, Raul wanted a drink.

He did not want to be standing in some draughty old castle, rowing with a woman he wanted—even after the way she had left—to have all over again.

Lydia turned him on.

And, titled or not, he turned *her* on too.

Raul could feel it.

This day might end not in bed but on the floor, two minutes from now.

But sex had got them into this hot mess and it was time for him to get out.

'Lawyer up!' he said, and turned and left.

He was leaving, Lydia knew.

Leaving their baby in the hands of lawyers.

She ran out and grabbed his arm.

'I'll talk to you.'

He looked down at her hand and shook it off, because even minimal contact he could not keep to for long.

'Then go and pack,' Raul told her. 'If you're not ready in five minutes we leave it to the professionals to sort out.'

She packed—though five minutes didn't give her much time. Especially when she wasted two of them by sitting on her bed and wondering what she should do.

She could not bear to go back to Venice.

Yet Lydia knew she had to.

Somehow she had to get past the raw hurt and sort out the future of their child.

He had hurt her so deeply, though.

And he didn't even know.

Just like the jagged wound that ran down Raul's back, just like the savage scar on Bastiano's cheek, her pain ran deep.

She had been used for revenge.

It was a wound that could never properly heal.

And yet Lydia knew she had to be adult and somehow work out terms with this difficult and complex man.

There was the baby to focus on, and she would not be weakened by his undeniably seductive charms. The sexual energy between them had unnerved her— Lydia was still aware of her palm where she had grabbed his arm.

But she dusted her hands together and brushed it off.

No way!

Worried that her mother might return and sell the statue, Lydia wrapped it in a thick jumper and packed it. Trying as she did so to not remember the night when it had been the two of *them* melded and heated. She swore she would not allow herself to lose her head to him again.

No, she would not weaken.

Lydia walked down the steps and he didn't rush to relieve her of her case. Instead he stood impatient at the door.

'Hold on,' she said, and bent down. 'I forgot to lock it.'

'For God's sake!' he said, and went over and took it. 'Come on.'

'Raul…' Lydia stalled. She wanted to make things very clear. 'I'm going to Venice only to discuss the baby.'

'What else would I be bringing you there for?' he asked. 'Lydia, you've had what you wanted from me in the bedroom department.'

'I just want to make it perfectly clear. I don't want—'

'Lydia, let me stop you there,' Raul interrupted her. 'This isn't about your wants—we're going to be discussing our child.'

'Well, let's keep things civil.'

'Civil?' Raul checked. 'I thought you didn't consider me capable.'

'I meant businesslike.'

'That,' Raul responded as they walked to the waiting helicopter, 'I can clearly be.'

'Good.'

He might just as well have painted her gold and handed her a spade as he stalked ahead with her case.

And the last word was his.

'But then, you knew that right from the start.'

CHAPTER FIFTEEN

THERE WAS NO worse place to be lonely than Venice.

And for Lydia that theory was proved again.

Loretta, his housekeeper, walked her along the lovely mirrored hallway, but instead of going straight ahead, Lydia was shown to the right.

She walked along another hallway and through to an apartment within his home. Loretta brought her dinner, and it was served at a polished table on beautiful china, but though her surroundings were gorgeous Lydia ate alone.

Raul, of course, ate out.

Naturally she didn't sleep, and in the morning she spent ages trying to work out what to wear.

It wasn't just that she had no idea what she should wear to a meeting to discuss their child's future. Nothing was a comfortable fit.

Lydia had no choice but to settle for the taupe dress—the one with the buttons. Only now it strained across her breasts.

Instead of undoing a couple of buttons she put on a little cardigan.

It would have to do.

She loathed it that she had been pencilled in as some sixty-minute item on his to-do list.

And she certainly hadn't expected an audience to be in attendance!

But as she walked into the drawing room Raul sat relaxed and chatting with a very beautiful woman.

'This is Allegra,' Raul told her. 'My assistant.'

Lydia, with her hackles already up and perhaps a little too used to her mother's handling of staff, gave Allegra a cursory nod and then ignored her.

Raul could see that Lydia was uncomfortable and he didn't blame her for that.

He had resisted discussing this at her home and was aware that he had the advantage, so he moved to the first point on his list.

'Would you be more comfortable in a hotel?'

'I don't intend to be staying very long,' Lydia replied coolly. 'The apartment is sufficient.'

Sufficient?

She had a six-room apartment within his home.

But Raul said nothing—just moved to the next point.

'There is a property less than a mile from here that has come onto the market. Allegra has arranged a viewing for you at two today.'

'Why would I need to see a property here?' Lydia asked. 'The baby will be raised in England.'

'But I shall be seeing my baby regularly. I assume you will want to be close when I do? Especially at first.'

'You assume correctly. However…'

But Raul had moved on.

'Allegra is going to look into the hiring of a nanny. It would appear good ones need to be secured early.'

That was an easy one, and Lydia dismissed it with a shake of her head. 'I shan't be hiring a nanny.'

It really annoyed her when Allegra wrote something down, and then she asked Lydia a question in a rich Italian purr.

'Will you want to sit in on the preliminary interviews, or would you prefer I do that and then we discuss the shortlist?'

'I just *said*...' Lydia was responding to Allegra as if she was speaking to a three-year-old with a hearing problem '...that I don't require a nanny.'

'We heard you the first time,' Raul said. 'But *I* need a nanny for the times when the baby is to be with me.'

Lydia, who had been glaring at Allegra, snapped her gaze back to Raul. 'Could we speak alone, please?'

'Of course.'

Allegra stood and walked out. Lydia sat with her back ramrod-straight and said nothing until the door behind her had closed.

Oh, but when it closed!

'You've been busy.'

'Yes,' Raul agreed.

And as she sat there she gleaned the fact that while she'd been eating alone last night Raul had been out to dinner, with Allegra, discussing her baby's future.

Of course he had.

Raul's time was heavily in demand, and a lot of his day-to-day stuff was delegated.

'Do you really think I have time to be wandering around looking at apartments for someone I spent a weekend with three months ago?'

Lydia opened her mouth to respond, but then closed it.

'You wanted businesslike, and you have made it clear you don't want to be in Venice for long, so I discussed things with my assistant...'

'Over *dinner*,' Lydia sneered. 'Have you slept with her?'

Oh, she hated it that she'd asked that—she really did.

'What the hell does that have to do with anything?'

And she hated his exasperated inevitable answer.

'Yes, but that was ages ago.'

And then he asked Lydia again.

'What the hell does that have to do with this?'

And she still couldn't answer, because really it should have *nothing* to do with this—yet it did.

'Lydia, I have a past—quite a colourful one. You really should choose your one-night stands more carefully.'

'I just don't like the fact...'

'Go on,' Raul said when she faltered, and he leant back in his chair to hear what she had to say.

'I don't like the fact that someone you've been intimate with is discussing my future and my baby.'

'*Our* baby.'

'Yes, but...' She tried to get back to the nanny point, because she was starting to sound jealous.

Which she was.

And irrational.

Which she wasn't.

Was she?

'Lydia, Allegra is very happily married.' He was annoyingly patient in his explanation. 'In fact I've already told you that. If you really think she's making bedroom eyes at me and we're still at it, then that's your issue. But we're not. I don't like cheats. Now, can we bring it back to business?'

'*It* is a baby.'

'*Che cazzo!*' he cursed.

'Don't swear.'

'The baby can't hear me!' Raul said.

'You discuss it so clinically.'

'You told me yourself to keep it businesslike. Come on, Lydia, tell me what you want. You've had three months to get used to the idea. I've had less than twenty-four hours. Tell me what you've decided and we can work from there.'

And she tried to tell him just that.

'There's no need for me to have an apartment here. Of course we'll visit often…'

A smile—a black smile—played on his lips, and she sat back as Raul chose his words.

'And where would you stay?' Raul asked. 'The guest wing?'

As she nodded that dark smile faded.

'Lydia, I don't want my ex, or rather one of my one-night stands, as a regular guest in my home. I don't want someone who has already said that she disapproves of me dictating the relationship I have with my child.'

'And I don't want my baby to be raised by a nanny.'

'Tough.' Raul shrugged. 'Do you *really* see me getting up at night to feed it and…' He pulled a face.

And, no, she could *not* see it.

'Raul, I haven't made any plans…'

'Oh, I would say you set your plans in motion a

long time ago,' Raul said. 'And I would suggest that
when you "forgot" to take your Pill you thought you'd
chosen carefully indeed.'

She frowned.

He enlightened her.

'I said I don't like children, and you decided I'd
make a very good absentee father...'

'No!' she shouted.

'Correct,' Raul said. 'Because I shan't just be a
chequebook father—I'm going to be very hands-on.'

He dismissed her then—she knew it from the wave
of his hand.

'We're getting nowhere. We can try again tomorrow if you would like?'

'You're going to schedule me in again?' Lydia
asked in a sarcastic tone.

Raul ignored it but answered her question. 'If you
want me to.'

And that was how they would be, Lydia was starting to realise.

Parents, but apart.

So, so far apart that she could not see across the
void.

'Do you want to see the apartment?' Raul checked
before he closed this disaster of a meeting. 'We should
try to get as much as possible done while you're still
here.'

'Fine.'

Raul heard the resignation in her voice and loathed
it.

They had ended up fighting, and he knew he tended
to win fights.

'I think perhaps we should do this through lawyers,' Raul admitted.

He didn't want to fight Lydia. He just wanted the details sorted. He would leave it to them and then sign.

'Raul, I can't afford a lawyer.'

It was a very difficult admission for someone like Lydia to make.

But he just sat there and leant back in his chair, and wondered just who she took him for.

'We both know that's not true.'

'Seriously, Raul. I know I live in a castle…'

'Lydia,' he told her as he sat there, and let her know himself how to nail him to the wall. 'Call a lawyer—the best you can find—and tell him my surname.'

'I can't afford to.'

'Try it,' he said. 'Tell them whose baby you're having and I guarantee they won't give a damn as to the current state of your finances. They'll probably offer to hold your hand in the delivery room.'

She stood.

'For their cut, of course,' Raul added.

He watched as she walked out, and usually he would be feeling delighted that a meeting had concluded early and he could get on to the next thing.

Yet she *was* the next thing.

When there was so much he should be getting on with Raul sat there thinking. Not even about the baby, but about her.

All roads did *not* lead to Rome.

But to Lydia.

Instead of thinking about the baby, which surely she should be, all Lydia could think about was Raul.

He was trying to get this sorted for both of them as best he could, Lydia thought as the realtor let both herself and Allegra into the apartment.

It was stunning, with crimson walls and drapes and a view of the canal.

In fact from one of the bedrooms she could see the balcony of his home.

'I missed that when I came this morning,' Allegra said when she looked to where Lydia's gaze fell, and again she wrote something down.

'Sorry?' Lydia checked.

'I'm sure you don't need a view of Daddy's home from yours! You'll want your own life...'

Allegra was trying too, Lydia realised.

Lydia was so used to everyone being the enemy.

No one really was here.

They were trying to do this without lawyers, and she was fighting them at every point, and Lydia knew why.

It wasn't the Venice apartment she wanted, nor the monthly payment dump in her account, or flights on his jet for time with Daddy.

It was Raul.

And for a tiny moment she had considered that desire attainable.

That was why she still held on to the statue—because when she'd opened up that box and looked down from the balcony for a second she'd thought it was possible that someone might actually *love* her.

Allegra was talking with the realtor, and then she excused herself to take a call on her phone.

From her affectionate tone, it was her husband, and

from what Lydia could glean they were discussing what they would have tonight for dinner.

She almost smiled as she recalled for the millionth time one of her and Raul's conversations.

Only she couldn't smile.

Because if they were a couple she'd be texting him now, or telling him tonight, and they'd be laughing at their own private joke.

But they weren't a couple.

And in that same conversation he'd told her he never wanted marriage.

She looked out to the canal. She was back where she had longed to be, but she ached at the coolness between them.

Lydia didn't just want the parenting side of things to be sorted.

There was a reason she was resisting everything he suggested and she faced the lonely truth—

Lydia wanted Raul, herself and the baby to be a family.

CHAPTER SIXTEEN

'Here.'

Loretta set down Lydia's dinner. Homemade fettuccini and a creamy sauce that smelt delicious. Finally Lydia's appetite was back.

'It looks lovely.'

'It is nice to have someone to cook for.' Loretta accepted the compliment. 'This is a recipe from Casta. I haven't made it for years.'

'You're from Casta?'

'I worked for Raul's father, and now for him. I know who I prefer.'

Lydia didn't respond at first. She assumed from that that Raul worked her too hard.

'I guess Raul must be demanding.'

'Raul?' Loretta laughed. 'No. I love working for him. It's been nearly ten years now, and I still pinch myself to make sure that it's true. I worked in his father's bar for more years than I care to count. Then Raul brought me to Rome and I used to take care of the apartments, and then I ran the housekeeping side of his first hotel.' She gave Lydia a smile. 'I'll leave you to eat.'

'Thank you,' Lydia said. Only she didn't want to

be left to eat—she wanted to chat with Loretta, and she wanted to know more about Raul, but it wasn't her place to ask.

What *was* her place?

Lydia didn't know.

And so she ate her dinner and had a bath, and then pulled on summer pyjamas which were short and a bit too tight, then lay in her bed in the guest room while no doubt Raul headed out.

Perhaps for another dinner to discuss her and the baby.

His latest set of problems.

And all because he wanted to get back at Bastiano!

Lydia didn't have the energy to think about that right now.

She was hurting.

They had to talk.

And, no, she didn't care if she was running outside his schedule and it wasn't her appointed hour.

They were *going* to discuss this.

Properly.

Even the difficult things, like nannies and visiting times.

She had no idea where in the house he was.

But she'd find him.

And if he wasn't at home...

She would wait.

Raul was actually in his office.

He looked up as Allegra stopped by on her way home and told him what she had organised.

'I've arranged two other apartments for Lydia to

look at tomorrow, and there's a courier coming to-morrow at nine.'

'A courier?'

'You said you had a package you wanted hand-delivered to Casta?'

'Oh, yes.'

'How did you find her in the end?' Allegra asked as she pulled on her coat. 'I think I visited maybe fifty castles and rang a hundred more.'

'She found me,' Raul replied.

Only that wasn't quite true. But he didn't run ev-erything by Allegra, and he certainly wasn't going to discuss the meeting he'd had with Bastiano with her.

With anyone.

'Anything else?' Allegra checked.

'I don't think so.'

She was gone.

And Raul didn't blame her a bit.

Last night she had worked till close to midnight, trying to have things as prepared as possible for today.

And tonight he had kept her again past ten.

'Raul?'

He looked up and there was Allegra, still hover-ing at the door.

'Yes?'

'I just thought I should let you know I'm also look-ing for a nanny.'

'Maybe hold back on that till Lydia has got more used to the idea.'

'I meant for me.'

'Oh,' Raul said, though what he really wanted to say was *merda*.

What the hell was going on with everyone?

'You're supposed to say congratulations.'

Raul rolled his eyes.

'I'm going to be running a crèche—I can see it now. Go home.'

'I am going. Seriously, though, it's going to be difficult finding a nanny who works to your hours. I don't want Lydia to explode in temper, but we really do need to start making some enquiries.'

'Leave it for now,' he said, and as Allegra walked off he wearily remembered his manners and congratulated her on the news of her baby. *'Complimenti!'*

Allegra just laughed as she walked out.

She knew he didn't mean it!

And her care factor?

Zero.

She really was a most brilliant PA.

But Allegra was wrong about one thing, Raul thought—Lydia didn't explode.

She imploded rather than let out the rage she held on to.

He'd seen it himself.

Whereas *he*…

Raul poured cognac and it was well earned—especially when he recalled how he had held on to his temper when Bastiano had insulted his mother.

But, no, that wasn't right.

It had been the truth that had held him back.

Bastiano had thought it was love between them.

Yet he had been just seventeen.

His mother had been in her mid-thirties.

What a mess!

Raul went into his drawer and took out the ring and went to package it for the courier.

Usually, of course, his parcels and such were left for others to deal with.

Not on this occasion.

This was beyond personal, Raul thought as he looked at the ring.

It was like holding a ghost—and one he didn't even know.

Bastiano was an orphan.

Had this been his mother's ring?

What the hell had his mother been doing, taking such a ring from a teenager?

A kid, really.

They had been children then.

Sure, they had thought they were adults, but what the hell…?

His mind leapt to the defence of the seventeen-year-old Lydia.

He was furious at how she'd been treated by adults who should have known better.

And now he sat trying to do the hardest thing in his life—afford Bastiano the same feelings.

'Raul!'

This time it wasn't Allegra.

Instead a very pale Lydia stood in the doorway, in short pyjamas.

He could see all the tiny changes in her. Her hips were rounder, her breasts fuller, but he wasn't really noticing them in reference to her being pregnant.

Her hips were round and her breasts were full and she would never, *ever*, not turn him on.

And how the hell did he keep his distance?

How did he keep removing himself from want?

He saw her gaze descend to the ring he held.

'Don't worry.' He did his best to keep things level and dropped the ring back in the drawer. 'I wasn't planning a surprise. It isn't for you.'

And to her shame, to the detriment of her stupid heart, for a second she had hoped that she might have found someone who would never leave.

Fool!

And when Lydia was angry, when she was hurting, she was ice.

'Of course it isn't,' Lydia said in her most crisp and affected tone, but then it cracked, just a little, and she could hold it in no more. 'You never cared about me—not for a moment. You were too busy working out how to get to Bastiano…'

'Merda.'

This time he said it out loud as he realised that she knew.

'Lydia!' Raul stood—not in defence, more in horror.

'Don't!' she warned him. 'Don't you *dare* try to justify it.'

'I'm not. How long have you known?'

'*I* get to ask the questions—did you follow me out of that dining room because you were interested in me or because you wanted to find out more about Bastiano?'

Before he could react, she took away the safe answer.

'And please don't say *both*, Raul—at least give me the truth.'

He owed her that.

'Bastiano.'

Absolutely the truth hurt, but she forced herself to speak on. 'And when you invited me for dinner was it to get to him? When you told me to choose…?'

She wanted to spit as she recalled it.

'Were you hoping to flaunt me in front of him?'

'Yes,' Raul answered, and he knew that the absolute truth was needed now. 'Because that's how I've always operated—that's how I have run my life. I lie to get by. I say what I have to. However—'

'I *hate* you!' Lydia shouted.

Oh, the ice hadn't cracked—it had split wide open. And fury was pouring out—years of it.

And it terrified her.

'You're the cheat, Raul! You say you hate them, but you're actually the cheat. You were lying all along.'

'Not all along.'

'Yes! You screwed me to get back at him!'

She walked out, and then she ran.

Back to her room.

The bed was turned down and the light was on and she wondered how it could look just as it had before, now he had told her himself the truth—he had pursued her to get back at Bastiano.

'Lydia.' He didn't knock, he just came in, and he was very calm.

'Get out.'

'No. We're going to talk about this.'

His head was actually racing—everything looked different now.

'When did you find out?'

'Does it even matter?'

Of course it did—and of course he knew when she had found out.

When everything between them had changed.

'You were right,' Lydia said, her temper rising. 'We'll do this through lawyers.' She meant it. 'I'm going to screw *you* now, Raul. I am going to make your life hell.'

'You couldn't.'

He took her arms and tried to calm her, but she was crying now—seriously crying.

'You couldn't make my life hell.'

Lydia took his words as a threat—that he was mightier, richer—but he meant it otherwise.

Hell was *not* having her in his life.

An angry Lydia he could deal with—was what he had waited for, in fact.

Because her fury was private and deep and finally she shared it.

Loudly.

'You lied.'

'I did,' Raul agreed. 'That's what my life was like until you came along.'

'You were using me.'

'At first,' Raul said, but then reconsidered. 'Actually, I wanted you on sight. I remember your buttons.'

'I don't take that as a compliment.'

'Take it any way you like. The floor is yours.'

His calm enraged her.

That he could just *stand* there when she'd exposed what he had done.

'I should never have told you about the baby.' She picked up the statue. 'I should have just sold this and you'd never have known.'

'I thought you already had sold it.'

And it had hurt him that she had.

Like her blasted mother—taking heirlooms and passing them on to get through another week.

He loved that statue too, and now she was holding it in her hand and about to toss it.

Raul stood there, a little conflicted.

He could stop her, because he knew she'd regret it later.

But she was angry.

Not just at him—that much he knew.

And, hell, she deserved to show it.

Lydia did.

She threw it.

Not at him.

She threw it against the wall and heard it shatter and she did the same.

Because she loved it, and she had destroyed the nicest thing she had ever had.

Except for Raul.

Yet she had never really had him at all.

And she wanted him so much.

But he didn't want her.

So why was he kissing her? Why was he telling her he'd better lock up the china or they were going to have very expensive rows?

Why, when she was crying and kicking and, oh, so angry, did he contain her, yet let her be, and seem to want her at the same time?

They were frantic—tearing buttons and shredding clothes with their lips locked, because Raul wanted to be out of his head too.

Today had been hell.

Yesterday too.

And all the weeks before that.

He wanted her badly.

Raul kissed her hard, pushed her to the wall, and

her bottom was bare in his hands, and her swaying breasts were stilled by his chest.

Lydia climbed him.

Even as Raul was preparing himself she was wrapping around him, and then she was safe in strong arms and being taken away.

It was rough and intense, and her face was hot and wet as he kissed her cheek on his way to finding her mouth.

And there was not a scream left within her as she climaxed—there wasn't even air in her lungs left to come out. Because he took everything she had and gave her more.

Everything raced to her centre as he thrust in deep and filled her. Her orgasm was so tight as he joined her in a climax that went on as hers faded.

She was calmed and coming down, watching the tension of his features and revelling in the feel of his final rapid thrusts.

And then thought returned, but the hurt did not.

At least not in the way it had been there before.

They were still kissing as he let her down. Standing in a war zone and yet safe and kissing.

And then she peeled back and peeked out and saw the glass on the floor.

'I broke our statue...'

Because that was what it was.

Theirs.

A diary of them.

And she had destroyed it.

'Why didn't you sell it?'

'I couldn't.'

And that meant so much to Raul.

She hadn't taken a single photo—Lydia, he knew, held on to nothing—yet she had been unable to let this go.

'And now I've destroyed it,' Lydia said, looking at all the shattered glass.

'No.' He picked it up from the floor and showed her that the beautiful couple were somehow intact, just minus the sheet.

'I hated that sheet,' Raul said. 'I didn't like to say so to Silvio. It's his art and all that, but I think he made a mistake.'

'He's a master of his craft!'

'Well, I think it looks better now.' Raul shrugged. 'Though the valuers might disagree.' He smiled at her. 'But you don't need them now, and we don't need lawyers.'

Lydia wasn't so sure.

She could not deal with Raul with her head.

One tryst and she craved more—one more night in his bed and she would be putty.

And she was scared to try to forgive him.

Lydia was scared of his lies—in that he was the master.

'Come to bed.'

She knew he meant his.

'Come on.'

And it scared her, not that she would take his crumbs...

But that she did.

CHAPTER SEVENTEEN

WRAPPED IN A sheet on Lydia's command, so as not to scare Loretta, they headed down the mirrored hall.

'She won't be here,' Raul said as they shuffled along with him holding the statue.

'Well, I'm not walking naked through your house.'

'*Our* house.'

Lydia ignored that. Instead she asked about Loretta.

'How come she works for you?'

'Because she was always good to me, and when my father died I knew she would be without work.'

'So you *do* have friends?'

'I guess.'

They were at his bedroom—back to where she had promised never to be.

It was even more beautiful the second time around.

'It's so gorgeous.'

'It's your room now.'

He saw her shoulders stiffen.

'I mean it.'

'Raul, can we talk about this tomorrow? There's still a lot to sort out.'

'It's sorted.'

'Raul, I'm here because you found out I was pregnant. I don't think that's an awful lot to base a relationship on.'

'Nor do I,' Raul agreed. 'I lived with my parents, after all. It's not just the baby.'

'Please don't just say the right thing. You're a liar, Raul.' She thought back to the plane, the first time they had flown here. 'I can't bear the thought of you *pretending* to care. That's what you've been doing all along…'

'Never.'

'You stand there and tell me you're speaking the truth and then straight away you lie.'

'When I held your hand I wasn't lying. When we took a taxi rather than my car I was caring for you then. And when we didn't have sex that first time…'

He thought back.

'For a second I considered how good it would feel to get back at him.'

And she let out a sob and a laugh, because he was being too painfully honest now.

'But then I stopped,' Raul reminded her. 'And by morning I could not let you leave.'

'You should have told me you knew Bastiano.'

'I know that,' Raul admitted. 'But I knew that if I did you'd leave. And you did.'

'Had you *told* me…' Lydia said, and then halted. He was right. Whichever way she might have found out, she'd have gone.

'I missed you so much.' Raul said.

Now she knew he was lying.

'So much that you did nothing to try to contact me until I called and told you I was pregnant?'

'Lydia, I didn't even know your surname. I've had Allegra scouring all the castles in England.

She didn't believe him and he knew it.

'Ask her.'

'She'll say what you tell her to.'

'I think,' Raul said, 'that I've finally found someone as mistrusting as me.'

'You had three months to find me, and yet on the same day I call you to say I'm pregnant suddenly you appear.'

'I was already on my way when I heard your message,' Raul told her. 'Here…'

He placed the now naked statue on the bedside table and then went to his drawer and took out a piece of paper with her name and address written on it.

'That's Bastiano's handwriting. I went to Casta to ask him.'

He handed it to her and Lydia looked at the paper. And she thought she would keep it for ever, because it told her that she *had* been missed.

'You went to Bastiano just for this?'

'Well, it wasn't for his company.'

'Did the two of you fight?'

'No,' Raul said. 'Nearly. He said he wanted a ring that had been left to me by my mother.'

'The ring you were looking at before?'

Raul nodded and got into bed, patted the space beside him for her to lie down with him.

'Hasn't he had enough from you?' Lydia asked as she climbed in. She really could not fathom his mother leaving half her legacy to a very young lover rather than leaving it all to her only son.

'It was a ring that he gave to her, apparently.'

'Oh.'

'He wanted it back in return for your address. I think it might have belonged to his mother. He's an orphan.' He made himself say it. 'He wasn't my mother's first affair.'

'How do you know?'

'Because I had been lying to my father to save her since I was a small child.'

And he had been lying to himself to save her memory since she'd died.

'Bastiano was just seventeen—half her age. Back then I thought we were men, and I hated him as such, but now...'

It felt very different, looking back.

'We were good friends growing up.'

'Could you be again?'

Raul was about to give a derisive laugh, but then he thought for a moment. 'I don't know...'

And it was nice to lie in bed talking with another person, rather than trying to make sense of things by himself.

'I think that my mother had problems for a very long time. Perhaps even before she was married. I don't even know if I'm my father's son.'

'Does it matter?'

'I think it did to him.'

'Is that why he beat you?'

He had never told her that Gino had given him those scars on his back, but it was clear now and Raul nodded.

And when he examined those times without hate and with her by his side things were easier to see.

His hand was on her stomach, and he could feel the

little bump. It was starting to sink in properly that he would be a father.

She felt his hand there and wondered at his thoughts. 'I'm not a gold-digger, Raul.'

'I know. I had to put that statue in your case, remember?' He had gone over and over that time.

'I don't think I took the Pill every day, even though my mother had insisted I should be on it. I had no intention of sleeping with Bastiano, and maybe I should have known I wasn't covered. I didn't think.'

'Lydia, you could have been wearing a chastity belt that night and I'd have rung for wire cutters. I could have insisted we use a condom. Have you told your mother about the baby?' he added.

'No.'

'When will you?'

'When I'm ready to.'

'I'm glad you told me first,' Raul said.

'She was a mess when I got back. I think losing my father finally caught up with her. She kicked Maurice out. She's staying at her sister's now. She's agreed the castle should go on the market.'

'Lydia. I'll look after your mother, but not *him*.'

Maurice he could never forgive.

Lydia lay in his arms and gave a soft laugh at the way he'd spoken of Maurice, but then she thought about what he'd just said about her mother.

'You don't have to do that.'

'Of course I do.'

'No, Raul, you don't.'

'We're going to be a family, Lydia. Marry me?'

She lay silent. She could feel his hand on her stomach and put her hand over his. Lydia knew how she felt about Raul. But she also meant what she'd said—a baby wouldn't save them.

'You don't even *like* children.'

'No, I don't,' Raul agreed. 'I'll like ours, though. Please believe that I'm not asking you to marry me because of the baby.'

'I know that.'

She *almost* did.

But by his own admission Raul was a manipulative liar, and there was still the tiniest niggle that he was simply saying the right things to appease her.

But then she thought of his look of horror when she had exposed him. So unlike Arabella, who hadn't even flinched at being caught.

He seemed so loath to hurt her.

She was scared, though, to believe.

And as her mind flicked around, trying to find fault with this love, Raul lay sinking into his first glimpse of peace.

That feeling—not quite foreboding, but almost—was fading. His constant wondering as to how she was had been answered. He thought of that first surge of jealousy when he'd thought that she and Bastiano might be lovers.

And now they lay there together and he looked at her. 'Were you jealous at the thought of Allegra and me?'

'Of course I was.'

'Are you now?'

'No.' She shook her head.

'She really was looking for you for weeks. And,' he added, 'I've just found out she's pregnant too.'

And then she knew she wasn't jealous any more,

or suspicious of Allegra, because he answered a question she wasn't even thinking.

'It's not mine.'

'I would *really* hope not.'

And he smiled, and when he did, for Lydia it was easy to smile too, but he could see the little sparkle of tears in her eyes on what should be their happiest night.

'Marry me?' he said again.

'Raul…'

Oh, she knew he cared—and deeply. And she knew how she felt. But there was still a tiny part of her that was scared that he'd asked in haste.

That without a baby there wouldn't be any 'them'.

She would just have to deal with it, Lydia knew. She would just have to accept never quite fully knowing if they were only together for the sake of their child. Because in every other way it felt perfect.

Stiff upper lip and all that.

'I hated being without you,' Raul said.

'And me.'

'No,' Raul said, 'I mean it. I felt as if there was something wrong. The sky seemed hung too low.'

He had been trying to work out what was wrong for months, and now suddenly, just like that, he knew exactly what had been wrong.

Raul had never felt it before.

Lydia lay looking at the chandelier struck by moonlight. The shutters were open and there was the sound of a gondolier singing beneath them on the canal.

And then she heard something.

Not a bell.

But something as clear as one.

And it struck right at her soul and she turned her face to the sound.

'I love you,' Raul told her.

It can be said many ways, but when it is said right it strikes so clear and so pure. And the sound and the feeling vibrates and lingers and lasts even when it must surely be gone.

It's never gone.

She had heard his truth.

This really was love.

EPILOGUE

THERE HAD BEEN one more lie that Raul had told her.

Raul *did* get up at night for his baby.

And he fed and changed her.

Serena had come into their lives four weeks ago, and so far it had proved the perfect name.

Yes, she was from Venice—or La Serenissima—but it was more for her nature that the name had been chosen.

They had been rewarded with such a calm baby.

Of course she cried—but she calmed easily when held.

And they loved her so much.

From her one blonde tufty curl to her ten perfect toes.

It was seven on a Sunday—Lydia knew that without opening her eyes because her favourite bell rang its occasional deep note and the others would join in soon.

Raul was speaking to Serena as they stood on the balcony, telling her she should go back to sleep.

It made Lydia's heart melt to watch the gentle way he held his daughter.

He was naked from the waist up and she could see his scars. She was grateful for them.

Sometimes she needed their reminder, because life felt perfect and the scars told her how far they had come.

Lydia closed her eyes as he turned around, pretending to be asleep.

'Shh...' Raul said as Serena let out a protest when he returned her to her crib.

Serena hushed, and after a moment of watching her sleep Raul got dressed.

Lydia wanted to protest and insist that he come back to bed.

Sunday was her favourite day.

Raul would go out from their room and return with the breakfast Loretta had prepared. They loved Sunday breakfast in bed.

Where was he going?

Lydia heard the elevator taking him down and then the engine of his speedboat.

Perhaps he had gone for coffee?

Raul did that now and then.

She had hoped he would not this morning.

She lay there listening to the bells and then rolled on her back and looked at the lights. Wherever he had gone she was happy.

So happy that she fell back to sleep and then awoke to his voice.

'Happy Birthday.'

He *had* remembered.

Lydia had dropped no clues and given no reminders.

She hadn't met a stranger that morning. Lydia knew she had met the love of her life. A man who had told her that there was no one in his life whose birthday he remembered.

Now he had two.

Raul held out a cardboard box tied with a red velvet ribbon which was vaguely familiar.

And then he told her where he had been.

'Baci in gondola,' Raul told her. 'Had you not chosen to walk out that morning you would have had these.'

He handed her the box and she opened it up.

'I was coming back to ask you to stay.'

'I know that now.'

And then she asked him something that she had not before.

'Would you have told me about Bastiano then?'

'No,' he said. 'Maybe later that night, but that morning I was definitely coming home to go back to bed with you.'

'Here.' He handed her the other box he was carrying. 'Your present.'

Lydia opened it up and she was reminded of just how much she was loved.

It was an album filled with stunning photos of the castle.

Exterior shots and also interior.

And as she turned the pages it was like stepping into each room and seeing it as it had once been when she was a child.

The castle would be opened to the public today.

With Raul's help, things had been turned around.

Valerie lived in a cottage on the grounds, and this afternoon would be taking the first visitors in a very long time through the glorious building.

But that wasn't all of Lydia's presents.

'We fly at ten,' Raul told her. 'Then we are having

afternoon tea in the garden. You'll make a gentleman of me yet.'

He *was* one.

A thousand times over and Lydia still cringed a bit when she thought of the words she had said, right here in this bedroom, that awful day.

They had survived it.

Better than that, they had thrived.

Raul came into the bed and they lay there, listening to the bells and to the contented sounds of their baby.

'When are we getting married?' Raul asked.

It hadn't yet happened.

'Soon.' Lydia smiled.

'You keep saying that,' Raul grumbled.

The last six months had been wonderful, but crazy. Their love had hit like lightning, and Lydia kept waiting to come down from the dizzy high and get organised.

She was starting to accept that there was no comedown when Raul was close.

Their kiss was slow, and he kept telling her he loved her, and then Raul rolled on top of her and told her that he was tired of waiting.

She felt him *there* and he smiled.

'I didn't mean for that.'

'I know you didn't,' Lydia said.

But it had been four weeks and she was ready now.

'You're sure?'

He was very slow and tender, and that was a side of Raul that even he was only starting to find out existed.

It was the best birthday she could have known. They made slow Sunday love and afterwards he stayed leaning over her and told her that there was another thing she did not know.

'Raul?'

'We get married today,' Raul said.

Lydia frowned.

They both wanted a small wedding and had thought about having it here in Venice.

Or Rome, where they had first met, perhaps?

Even Sicily, for together they had been back there.

'At the castle,' Raul said.

That had been but a dream, for it had been falling down around them when they'd first met.

It was beautiful now.

'Yes?' he checked.

'Yes!' Lydia said.

'Per favore?' Raul said, and took her right back to the day they had met.

'Yes, please!' Lydia said, and together they smiled.

She *had* chosen wisely, for Raul was the love of her life.

And he would be King.

* * * * *

#3517 THE DESERT KING'S CAPTIVE BRIDE
Wedlocked!
by Annie West

Princess Ghizlan is stunned when Sheikh Huseyn seizes her late father's kingdom. Her captor is intent on taming her fierce pride—and making her his own! It won't be long before they fall prey to the firestorm between them...

#3518 HIS MISTRESS WITH TWO SECRETS
The Sauveterre Siblings
by Dani Collins

After her fling with Henri Sauveterre ends, Cinnia Whitley discovers she's carrying twins! Dare she keep it a secret? Henri is furious at Cinnia's deception—but *any* Sauveterre deserves his protection. Can Henri prove how *pleasurable* their reunion will be?

#3519 CROWNED FOR THE DRAKON LEGACY
The Drakon Royals
by Tara Pammi

One night with Mia Rodriguez is all that daredevil Prince Nikandros will allow himself before he faces his royal duty. But when their sizzling liaison leads to an unexpected pregnancy, Nik won't rest until he claims his child—*and* his princess!

#3520 THE ARGENTINIAN'S VIRGIN CONQUEST
Claimed by a Billionaire
by Bella Frances

Lucinda Bond's aloofness hides insecurities so painful that she's never allowed herself to be touched. But Dante Hermida's caressing gaze ignites a desperate desire. It's soon clear Dante longs to claim her...with a need that shows no sign of abating!

YOU CAN FIND MORE INFORMATION ON UPCOMING HARLEQUIN® TITLES, FREE EXCERPTS AND MORE AT WWW.HARLEQUIN.COM.

HPCNM0317RB

*Raul Di Savo desires more than Lydia Hayward's
body—his seduction will stop his rival buying her!
Raul's expert touch awakens Lydia to irresistible
pleasure, but his game of revenge forces Lydia to leave...
until an unexpected consequence binds them forever!*

Read on for a sneak preview of
Carol Marinelli's 100th book,
THE INNOCENT'S SECRET BABY,
the first part of her unmissable trilogy
BILLIONAIRES & ONE-NIGHT HEIRS.

Somehow Lydia was back against the wall with Raul's hands
on either side of her head.

She put her hands up to his chest and felt him solid
beneath her palms and she just felt him there a moment and
then looked up to his eyes.

His mouth moved in close and as it did she stared right
into his eyes.

She could feel heat hover between their mouths in a slow
tease before they first met.

Then they met.

And all that had been missing was suddenly there.

Yet the gentle pressure his mouth exerted, though blissful,
caused a flood of sensations until the gentleness of his kiss
was no longer enough.

A slight inhale, a hitch in her breath and her lips parted,
just a little, and he slipped his tongue in.

The moan she made went straight to his groin.

At first taste she was his and he knew it for her hands moved to the back of his head and he kissed her as hard as her fingers demanded.

More so even.

His tongue was wicked and her fingers tightened in his thick hair and she could feel the wall cold and hard against her shoulders.

It was the middle of Rome just after six and even down a side street there was no real hiding from the crowds.

Lydia didn't care.

He slid one arm around her waist to move her body away from the wall and closer into his, so that her head could fall backward.

If there was a bed, she would be on it.

If there was a room, they would close the door.

Yet there wasn't and so he halted them, but only their lips.

Their bodies were heated and close and he looked her right in the eye. His mouth was wet from hers and his hair a little messed from her fingers.

"What do you want to do?" Raul asked while knowing it was a no-brainer, and he went for her neck.

She had never thought that a kiss beneath her ear could make it so impossible to breathe let alone think.

"What do you want to do?" He whispered to her skin and blew on her neck, damp from his kisses, and then he raised his head and met her eye. "Tonight I can give you anything you want."

Don't miss
THE INNOCENT'S SECRET BABY,
available March 2017 wherever
Harlequin Presents® books and ebooks are sold.

HARLEQUIN

Presents.

Coming soon—the first part of Bella Frances's sizzling debut duet for Harlequin Presents, Claimed by a Billionaire! Don't miss *The Argentinian's Virgin Conquest*, a simmering story of irresistible temptation…

Lucinda Bond might be descended from English nobility, but her aloofness hides painful insecurities. Painful enough that she's never allowed herself to be touched.

Then Dante Hermida sweeps her from the Mediterranean Sea, mistakenly thinking she's drowning, and suddenly Lucie finds herself in the arms of Argentina's most outrageous playboy! His arrogance challenges her boundaries, but his caressing gaze ignites a desperate desire…

Despite Lucie's defiant facade, soon Dante has her utterly at his sensual command! But after discovering Lucie's innocence, this dark-hearted Argentinian finds himself longing to claim her… with a need that shows no sign of abating!

Don't miss
THE ARGENTINIAN'S VIRGIN CONQUEST
Available April 2017

And look out for
THE ITALIAN'S VENGEFUL SEDUCTION
Available May 2017

Stay Connected:
www.Harlequin.com

 /HarlequinBooks

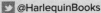 @HarlequinBooks

 /HarlequinBooks

HP06060

Get 2 Free Books,
Plus 2 Free Gifts—
just for trying the Reader Service!